I0761273

PLANET EARTH

PRAISE FOR NICHOLAS RUDDOCK'S NOVELS

Night Ambulance

"Nicholas Ruddock strips away the politics and policies that have trapped and defined women for decades and gets to the heart of the people who live with these decisions. [He] reveals a world controlled by men … and the women who navigate this system … Ruddock's tense warning could easily be a vision of the future in a novel as poignant as it is painfully hopeful." —Lindsay Raining Bird, *Atlantic Books Today*

The Parabolist

"Comic and inventive." —*Edmonton Journal*

"*The Parabolist* has a strong push that will keep your heart beating until the end." —*The Globe and Mail*

"Dazzling … an exciting, compelling, and expertly layered mystery." —Anthony De Sa, author of *Children of the Moon*

"Passionate, offhand, deeply charming and deeply original." —Damian Tarnopolsky, author of *Every Night I Dream I'm a Monk, Every Night I Dream I'm a Monster*

Last Hummingbird West of Chile

"Have you ever read an author whose voice is so potent that your own voice bends to it, takes on its rhythms and syntax? And so you proceed through your day hearing events narrated in the voice of this newly discovered author who has you under his or her spell? This is what happened to me reading *Hummingbird.*" —Jessica Grant, author of *Come, Thou Tortoise*

"Boldly conceived, richly imagined, wondrously multi-vocal and unexpectedly comic … the perfect historical novel for a world just waking up to the realization that every living and non-living thing is vitally connected." —Padma Viswanathan, author of *The Charterhouse of Padma*

PLANET EARTH

STORIES

NICHOLAS RUDDOCK

Copyright © 2025 Nicholas Ruddock

Published in Canada in 2025 and the USA in 2025 by House of Anansi Press Inc.
houseofanansi.com

All rights reserved. No part of this publication may be reproduced or transmitted in any form or by any means, electronic or mechanical, including photocopying, recording, or any information storage and retrieval system, without permission in writing from the publisher.

House of Anansi Press is committed to protecting our natural environment. This book is made of material from well-managed FSC®-certified forests, recycled materials, and other controlled sources.

House of Anansi Press is a Global Certified Accessible™ (GCA by Benetech) publisher. The ebook version of this book meets stringent accessibility standards and is available to readers with print disabilities.

29 28 27 26 25 1 2 3 4 5

Library and Archives Canada Cataloguing in Publication

Title: Planet Earth : stories / Nicholas Ruddock.
Names: Ruddock, Nicholas, author
Identifiers: Canadiana (print) 20250172461 | Canadiana (ebook) 20250172488 | ISBN 9781487013561 (softcover) | ISBN 9781487013578 (EPUB)
Subjects: LCGFT: Short stories.
Classification: LCC PS8635.U34 P53 2025 | DDC C813/.6—dc23

Cover design: Alysia Shewchuk
Cover image: *Landfire* by Cheryl Ruddock
Interior design and typesetting: Lucia Kim

House of Anansi Press is grateful for the privilege to work on and create from the Traditional Territory of many Nations, including the Anishinabeg, the Wendat, and the Haudenosaunee, as well as the Treaty Lands of the Mississaugas of the Credit.

Canada Council for the Arts Conseil des Arts du Canada

With the participation of the Government of Canada
Avec la participation du gouvernement du Canada | Canada

We acknowledge for their financial support of our publishing program the Canada Council for the Arts, the Ontario Arts Council, and the Government of Canada.

Printed and bound in Canada

Cheryl, the cover painting, the flames

CONTENTS

WOLVERINE

THERE ARE COBRAS IN PERU. They're in the long grass by the river or in dried-out arroyos. They sway to their own rhythm, to the rhythm of the wind, to the slow quotidian rotation of the earth. They hug the dampness of loam, the chalk-dry dust. They regurgitate the bones of mice and feral dogs. Born in deep holes in the ground, they are several centimetres long at birth and have hundreds of brothers and sisters fighting for space, writhing together in seething balls, clustered. Most inevitably die, but one or two survive and leave the nest and thereafter live on their own. They are quick and merciless and, we assume—by measuring the size of their brains—that they react instinctively. That's anthropomorphism, however; perhaps they calculate every move at a speed beyond our own abilities or reasoning.

Why do I tell you this? Because of Mario Vargas Llosa.

I was born in Peru, as he was, twenty years before me. So we share a birthplace, and, of course, that singular locale bestows a similarity to our early years. But ultimately it is the divergence in our lives that commands attention. Well, it commands my attention, not his. He is world-famous as a writer, and I am not. He entered politics and rubbed shoulders with dictators, I did not. He won the Nobel Prize, I did not. Should I go on? He etcetera and I etcetera, our lives so different, more so as the years advanced. But we forged a bond once, on the night he struck Gabriel García Márquez in the face with his intemperate fist, and since then we have had a connection, of which he is unaware. No blame can be laid at his feet for what happened much later, in Toronto, Canada. He wasn't there, but a famous man can become, unwittingly, a mentor to violence.

I shall explain. At the age of seventeen, having led a normal youthful life, I was accepted to the Universidad Nacional Mayor de San Marcos, in Lima. There I met and became enchanted with a dark-haired girl named Estella. At that time, she accentuated her equally dark eyes with half-moons of kohl, and she was a fledgling member of the Communist Party. Her father, a banker, and her mother, a dressmaker, were not enthused with her politics or with me, her new boyfriend. They were distantly polite, that's all. But at my house, things were different. My parents were shocked and frightened and said directly to us, "What can you be thinking of, Eduardo? And you, Estella? By now the secret police will have your name, Estella, and therefore Eduardo's by association, and it is our money, earned by what you would call *bourgeois labour,* saved over the years in the safe banks of capitalism, that have allowed you to waste your time in cafés, both of you. Also to skip classes and to foment class warfare."

Estella and I stood together, holding hands, trying not to respond in an inflammatory way.

"Eduardo," they continued, "you say you are in love with this girl, against whom we have nothing but whose parents must feel the way we do—betrayed. Look about you, both of you! You do this from the comfort of our large home in a neighbourhood of affluence from a bedroom with lace curtains and high ceilings, in which, by the way, you seem to have no concept of physical restraint."

When Estella was not present, my mother and father continued to harangue me, at our table, over roast pork or beef or fish from the sea, saying the two of us would inevitably be targeted and punished by the state, that Estella was bent on self-destruction, that she would take down those in her retinue with her. They had seen it often, proud and ancient families ruined. My mother also said that she had heard, through the grapevine of mothers and grandmothers, that Estella Sepulveda had many lovers, taking them indiscriminately. I should be wary of transmitted disease, she said. I shuddered at the thought but knew it was not true. In many ways, in her intimacies, Estella was shyer than I, more innocent.

Our parents took action. They joined forces at the end of the school year and, for the summer, she was banished to Paraguay, I to Mexico. Before we left, we met briefly at a café by the seawall to say goodbye. Pigeons ate disconsolate crumbs and gulls stalled overhead. Poets in chairs tilted forward, their hair slicked back, their faces chiselled. Anorexic were the women, bearded the men.

"We are to be exiled like Trotsky," she said.

"I'm the one who has to go to Mexico, therefore I am Trotsky, not you."

She looked at me with those sad, dark eyes.

"Trotsky was killed in Mexico with an axe. By an assassin. He was targeted. The same could never happen to us," she said.

I laughed. I knew nothing about the world of intrigue, assassination. My life was not in danger, and those facts, how Trotsky died, by axe, the details, were news to me.

"Estella! I am too supple to receive blows from an axe! Too quick! Look at me, for two months I shall work in my cousin's cinema, then we shall be reunited."

"We are being torn from our native roots."

"Do you think this café is under surveillance, Estella? My parents say it is."

She looked about, her eyes moving from the street to the waiters, the customers, then to me.

"Of course," she said.

Estella, the café, the sea, the birds, the secret police. Our life was thrilling. But we were also children of our parents, and obedient, so our summer separation would become a fact.

"We should not write," she said, "our letters will be opened. I am unable to prevaricate or dissemble. It does not matter, our love is inviolable."

We leaned across the table and kissed in full view of the spies, who were no doubt inwardly writhing in jealousy.

In Mexico City, I was given a room in the house of our cousins, on the second floor. My window overlooked extensive gardens. There was perfume in the early morning from flowers I could not name. A slow breeze shifted through the curtains, soft and pliant. I did not notice the notorious smog of the city until I was out in the street, mornings, walking to the bus stop. Then my throat would go dry as it never had in Lima, where fog smoothed the edges of rush hour, where the traffic lights blurred like watercolours, as though they were subaquatic, in yellow, green, and red.

I thought of her, the way she looked up from her books, her manifestos, her pamphlets, and even more so the way she threw her clothes to the floor saying, "Now our bodies are in service to the state."

"What do you mean by that?" I had asked.

"Eduardo, this is how the proletariat is formed." Then she laughed, which in my heart made me wonder, as I touched her, if I should question her sincerity. For in private, I admit, I questioned my own. Society had been under siege for so long, yet nothing seemed to change.

Those mornings in Mexico, I alighted from the number 52 bus between 8:58 and 9:02. I passed a kiosk, an apothecary, a bakery, and then I opened the door to the theatre, which was situated on a busy corner. The key was large, heavily toothed, cumbersome. It required some hand-jiggling and subtlety before the tumblers gave way to the lobby, the morning hush.

"Show up, be well-groomed, take tickets. Nothing could be simpler, Eduardo my nephew. Check the washrooms, there's a mop in the closet."

Those were my instructions. My uniform was of simple grey material with red piping and there was a hat, fez-like without a tail, which I was shown how to wear.

"Like this, Eduardo, see? This angle? Jaunty."

I was given a bobby pin to use in case it slipped.

"Tear tickets in half like this, when ushering please use this gesture with your arm—like so!—welcoming."

Two gold stanchions were joined by a scalloped rope, the rope as scarlet as the lipstick of the Hollywood actresses portrayed on the posters outside, pouting, smiling fetchingly, or knowingly, or both. Every one of our tickets had five digits stamped onto it in the same deep red. Also scarlet-red were the carpets and the heavy curtains and the wallpaper, though the wallpaper was decorated with gold filaments in an abstract pattern, meaningless.

"You are an eye on the street, Eduardo, and as you can see the neighbourhood is in decline, there is random violence, but in our cinema we are left alone, as a general rule. Crime rarely touches us. We portray magic, how the world should be, even for criminals. To be forthright, they are some of our best customers."

The outside world was a hectic arm's length away. Inside, the reels unwound, the soundtrack rose and fell like waves of a distant sea, muffled, foreign. The voices of the actors—this

I would have written to Estella had she allowed an exchange of letters—"were like syrup or castanets, smooth and desultory then staccato amidst laughter false and true," and there was shouting and the firing of guns and a crying or crying out, most often in English, a language I did not understand.

If you had told me that I would meet Mario Vargas Llosa there, that my life would be changed, I would have laughed. How ludicrous.

But one day my cousin said, "Eduardo, my friend, economic necessity dictates that the movies we show are fluff. You can see that. We pander that we may eat. However, for the upcoming festival, I have arranged to show films only by the Swedish director Bergman. Once a year we have this opportunity to show cinema as it can be, as genius. But he can be depressing, Bergman, even as he strikes to the heart—some would say the breaking heart—of love."

"Yes, cousin."

For the festival, the clientele changed. Men in dark suits arrived with young women in gowns, and smooth was the silk caressing the bodies of those ladies, tempting the whimsy of thin cotton. Estella, Estella, my thoughts were of her. The scarlet rope and the gold stanchions were pressed into service for the first time, for crowd control. Cigarette smoke filled the lobby, spilling from throats and tongues and heads tossed back. Small cigars were ground down and bent into white sand, into pedestal ashtrays we had polished for the occasion. Banks of flowers appeared too, erupting from vases of coloured glass. The background music changed into something more sombre, off-key, northern.

"May I have your tickets, please," I said again and again, "thank you." I fancied myself, for those few days and nights, as Hermes, conductor of souls to the underworld, gatekeeper to an inner sanctum where truth, for once, stumped artifice.

Those exact words I wrote to her by hand, breaking our pact of silence. To my surprise she replied, fondly, ignoring the censors, "Eduardo, you are learning so much about inequality from decadent intellectuals, and the quality of your writing is ever so much better. I love you. Do not write again."

Then it happened. On the second night of the festival, just before the screening of *Cries and Whispers*, Mario Vargas Llosa stepped into the lobby. The most famous writer in the Americas, a latecomer, unmistakably him, it could be no one else, alone. Casually, I took his ticket as though this happened to me daily, evincing no surprise. But I did say—and here I quoted from Herman Hesse—"Price of admission your mind, sir," and he laughed and stopped in his headlong rush. We compared our Peruvian accents, our neighbourhoods in Lima. Then a reedy note from within, the expiration of a solo accordion in E minor, and Mario Vargas Llosa said, "Excuse me, but Bergman..." and he shook my hand, and in he went, and the lobby was empty.

The ticket seller from outside left her booth, smiling at the take. She was holding a thick sheaf of pesos.

"Eduardo," she said, "soon our bosses will be even more millionaires."

Together we stood looking into the street at the rising quarter-moon, the passing kaleidoscope of cars, buses, sirens, heat. Her shoulder touched mine, then moved away. I thought again of Estella, wondering where she was, and with whom. I declined a cigarette.

Intermission came. The second film was to start in twenty minutes, *Shame*, from 1967. I saw Vargas Llosa in a knot of conversation by the outer door when "Mario!" came a shout. Everyone heard it, a greeting with such pleasure yet command, and all turned to see a shorter man, moustachioed, in a white linen suit, picking his way through the crowded lobby, his arms held open for an embrace.

But no welcome came.

"You son of a bitch!" Vargas Llosa said, and he struck the still-smiling and unsuspecting newcomer with his right fist, delivered straight from the shoulder in the classic stretched-out boxer pose. A cracking sound like eggs or bone jumped out of either the fist or the face, and, quivering now with his own violence partially spent, Vargas Llosa watched his victim fall backwards to the floor.

"García Márquez!" he shouted that all could hear, "how could you do this, to me, to Patricia? Get up you blowhard egotist!"

Then, laughing at some fiction or fact that only he could understand, he drew back his polished boot and kicked the already-dazed man—flapping hands splayed out in front in useless supplication—in the ribs. Once, twice, three times.

"*Hunghh-humph*," gasped the Colombian writer, for it was certainly he, also unmistakable, also apparently alone.

Vargas Llosa looked at me.

"Strike like a cobra, dear boy of Peru," he said, "this is how it is done."

I stepped up. It was my ground, my territory. Respectfully, I nudged Vargas Llosa to the side and knelt to the wounded. From his nose came a slow snuffling-pulsing ooze of dark blood, viscous, falling to the floor, and here the floor was tiled in a picturesque mosaic a century old. His blood dripped down upon a jungle tableau of green and yellow snakes seething in concert, also upon parrots squadroned across a muddy river, upon a jaguar's face black with jewelled eyes, supine upon a branch. Márquez's suit coat itself was smeared with red semi-clotted mucous, as was the collar of his open shirt, his mustache, a small pool gathering at the base of his throat.

"No more, no more," he managed to say.

By then other theatregoers had intervened. The confrontation was over and done with. Lights in sconces flicked off and on, beckoning all to the inner theatre. By then the beaten man was back on his feet. His left eyebrow was swollen and abraded, and he held a shaky shirt cuff muffled to his nose.

"I'm okay, I'm okay."

Smiling then as though nothing had happened, a brave face still stunned, concussed.

"Can you go back in?" I asked.

"Of course. I am here for the art of Bergman, not for this."

I held him fast by the elbow. He was wobbling and would have fallen had I not supported him to a back row seat. By then the house lights were dropping and the word "Shame" leapt subtitled to the screen. That simple word, so apt under the circumstances, resonated with all of us. Faces of concern looked our way. Several handkerchiefs travelled hand to hand in gestures of universal sorrow. As for Vargas Llosa, he had disappeared, gone with his devils or his angels, whichever they were, gone with his intemperance, his cobra strike.

Afterwards, as I emptied the ashtrays and vacuumed the carpets and mopped up the drying blood from the tiles, what I remembered most of this extraordinary night was the power of the Peruvian writer's anger, the spontaneity, the no-shame of it, the fierceness, the fire of his eye, the violence unleashed without restraint. Revenge was the only explanation. The patience and then the impatience, the knowledge of coiled strength, the recognition of the moment.

The rest of the summer passed quickly. Then I was back in Lima, and Estella was waiting at the airport. We kissed and went straightaway to a meeting of the Marxist League. I moved from my parents' house, and with our summer earnings we rented a small flat near the university. Now we were free of overt criticism. We lay together in joy and fascination every night in a bed with a cool breeze that felt its way over the rooftops from the sea. It wasn't long before she was pregnant because, Estella said, "the concept of birth control is foisted on the poor by the rich, the ruling class fear the young for their fecundity." She wrote pamphlets on this theme and distributed them on the street. When our first child was born, poverty dictated that we leave the university. The cost of books alone was prohibitive. We had to take jobs to support our family and were proud to do so. She wrote articles for her magazines while I found work in a public library, whistling under my breath as I stocked the shelves, looking quickly at new publications, especially those for small children. I stopped my own writing endeavours, my style seemed old-fashioned. Better I should stick, I thought, to the simple honesty of labour.

Then the government convulsed and changed direction and looked at Estella more carefully. They did not like what they saw. Men without uniform stopped her on street corners. They advised her to mend her ways. Our small and beaten-up car, upon which we depended, caught fire for no reason. We were denied proper insurance. By then we had three children, but Estella could still not be silenced. To bend her knee, she said, was anathema. I thought of Vargas Llosa, what he would do, but my hands were tied, and the enemy were phantoms. Any cobra strike would soon be traced back to us, and the children would suffer. I stayed my hand, I bowed my head.

"Eduardo, we have no choice but to leave the country."

Thus came the first sign of our eventual supplication. It took months for our paperwork to be processed, considered, rejected, processed again, reconsidered, stamped, reviewed, and finally approved. I was discharged from my job at the library. Bile rose in my throat, bile that could have been venomous but out of fear was instead pathetic, corrugating, a burning dagger in the chest harmful only to myself.

"Never mind," she said, "soon we will leave. Things will be better in Canada."

Canada had been the only country to accept us, but still we had to wait. During this time our children were expelled from primary school. They spent time only with similarly carefree children of other radicals. I watched them in the parks, running through fountains, shirtless, kicking balls into phantom nets. Meanwhile Estella took in laundry and rode a bicycle through the humid streets, delivering newspapers. This allowed her to say goodbye to her friends without compromising them, but her so-called friends were shying away.

"Eduardo, no longer do they invite me into their apartments. They look past me, scanning the hallways, they look everywhere but at me."

"Times have changed, Estella."

"They say goodbye, but they say it awkwardly. They're not sorry to see me go."

In October, she rode her bicycle up and down the familiar

hills for the last time. The rain-slicked cobbles were less treacherous, she said, than the words and sentences and paragraphs she had written in her manifestos. Nevertheless, twice she fell, and afterwards she chose to display her bruises as trophies, as substitutes for her waning political fearlessness.

Everything we could take with us fit into three suitcases. Unseen by the eyes of the neighbourhood, we waited for our cab in the shadowy vestibule of the apartment building. Dust motes in yellow sun canyoned down from the transom, and the children cried ensemble. At the airport were mirrored sunglasses on the faces, implacable, of the security police. Their reflections multiplied in the polished glass of vast windows. We spoke not a word in our depressed state, walking silently out onto a tarmac vaporous with jet fuel. A drizzle from low clouds mocked us, but the children were at least happier now, hand in hand, skipping, singing in rhymes. It was a lark for them.

"Airplane, airplane!" they said.

In Toronto, snow bristled in the air. We had no resources and the little money we'd saved vanished, becoming two months' rent for a small upstairs flat on Markham Street, south of College. After weeks of numbed paralysis and worry, Estella was hired as a cleaner by an employment agency.

"Eduardo, it has come to this."

"Yes."

"Nothing is different here. We will be subjugated with impunity by the same forces of capitalism, by platitudes and the minimum wage instead of by car fires, guns, and helicopters."

The employment agency dressed her in blue-grey overalls and wrote her first name, *Estella*, in yellow script above her left breast. The tools of her trade were a plastic bucket and a mop. She left home as unfamiliar dusk descended upon the northern streets, the sun slanting down from a more acute angle, and earlier in the day. Dark shadows jutted over curbs. Rarely did she raise political issues, or pronounce directly on the obvious inequalities we could see at every hand. It was as though she were now half-beaten. On Dundas Street, the children and I watched her climb aboard the streetcar, adjust her mop, shift the empty bucket at her feet. One of a crew of twenty in a skyscraper of metal and glass, she started every night at the fifty-sixth floor and descended, one paper-strewn level after the next. It could be peaceful there in the hum of the fluorescent lights and, for the most part, she was left to her own devices. And she was proud, she told me—as she had been in Lima with the newspapers and the bicycle and the laundry—to experience first-hand the life of a cleaning woman, after being raised in such comfort. She worked hard. She was praised by her supervisor for her fastidiousness, for never scuffing or chipping the legs of expensive furniture.

Then I was hired by the same company, but on a different shift. One of us was always at home with the children, walking them to school, watching them play on swings in the park, even in the ice and snow.

But I did not thrive as well as she did in the heart of capitalism. I found myself indifferent, even resentful as I scrubbed the porcelain bowls of toilets with cleanser and a bent-wire brush. Here the water in toilets was a false blue colour, from a cylinder in the tank, as though even our most natural functions needed a mask, a disguise. As Estella had done, I hoovered conference rooms and Lemon-Pledged mahogany until I could see a blurred version of my face reflecting back. I looked tired and older, and my supervisor upbraided me, "Faster, faster, Mr. Ariza, or whatever your name is, faster!" and he pushed me, slightly, between the shoulder blades, toward the public washrooms on the thirty-second floor. Just a push but I felt the familiar bile rise in me and, in my helplessness, I turned and pushed him back, not in the fashion of Mario Vargas Llosa but gently, and also saying, in an injured voice, "Don't touch me like that!" I could have been a child in a schoolyard, cowering. Tears filled my eyes. Then I turned away from the confrontation and stood alone for five minutes, ashamed, outside the empty washroom until my heart stopped beating its fandango.

I was terminated the next day, and so was Estella.

"Guilt by association, Eduardo. We need to learn better how to channel our personal discontent," she said.

I admitted to her how embarrassed I was by my passivity, how different my action had been from the crack of fist on face, in Mexico City, ten years before.

"I should have punched him hard. Better to be hanged as a wolf than a sheep."

"No, Eduardo. Here, if you do that, you will be arrested. Remember, we have children. And look, to be practical, now we need milk from the store."

I tucked my shirt into my pants, picked up my wallet from the kitchen table and took to the stairway. On Markham Street, I saw Canadian pigeons head-bobbing, beaking up whatever they could by the curb. Invisible scraps, pebbles. They appeared to have no responsibilities, certainly no children. At the store on Dundas, I didn't have enough change.

"Twenty-five cents short, what do you know. I'll be right back," I said, blushing.

The clerks rolled their eyes.

At home, Estella counted out what was left in her purse, turned out her pockets, and I returned to the store, to the eye-rollers. Later that night for the first time, my little former-Marxist cried. She no longer wore makeup of any kind. She held her fingernails knuckled into her hand. I stood and put my arms around her and held her head to my chest. I leaned down and kissed her hair. She was worn out by her labour.

"Those bastards in skyscrapers," she said.

Now we were even reusing tea bags, squeezing them in our fists, marinating them in water to make them last until there was no colour, no discernible taste.

"Oh, Eduardo," she said, "schoolbooks, crayons, binders, boots, coats, mittens. I'm going to talk to Juan Antonio up the street, maybe he has something."

And Juan Antonio said, "Yes, actually, Estella, if you don't mind driving and you don't mind evening work and you don't complain to me about social injustice, I do have a job for you."

"I will do whatever I must to make ends meet."

"Good. Then you take my car, you deliver pizza, you get five dollars a delivery."

"Five dollars?"

"In this relationship of ours, Estella, I am the capitalist, and you are the underclass. Why? Because I am the one with the means of production, namely the car. Which is capital. Every pizza you deliver, we split the take, which is ten dollars. Oh, you have to pay for gas. Even your friend Lenin would have to pay for gas, if he worked for me. There's a Shell station around the corner, as you may have noticed."

She reached out her hand and caught the car keys, which Juan Antonio threw in an easy loop across the kitchen table. He was fond of her despite his jibes.

At this juncture, I stayed home full-time with the children. My English was somehow much better than hers, and they needed help with homework. I put on a jolly front to fool them. They were as happy as clams. I remember their teacher saying to me exactly that, "They are as happy as clams, Mr. Ariza."

Her borrowed car was a small blue Kia with a plug-in sign glowing on the roof. But, as it turned out, delivering pizza was a tough job, even tougher than cleaning office buildings. There was no downtime at all. After she left the tiny bakery, its windows misted up with yellow light, heat from the ovens pumping in waves out the door onto Clinton Street, after she slid the pizzas into their insulated boxes, she didn't have time to amble along. Far from it, she had to race against the clock. Twenty minutes or the pizza was free. What? This was a shock to her, this unfortunate fact that Juan Antonio had forgotten to mention despite his enthusiasm for the market economy, which, he had said, "provides us with a ladder up, Estella." And the cost of the pizza, should she fail to deliver it on time, was twelve dollars from her own pocket. Plus the wasted gas. Thus, inevitably, did the humble worker pay.

There was a clock that glowed green on the dashboard of the Kia. She told me how she knuckled down on the steering wheel, stick-shifted her way through the narrow streets of downtown, accelerated through green lights and amber lights, revved impatiently at reds, double-parked, flipped on hazards, jumped out with still-warm boxes against her hand, raced up and down sidewalks checking out the numbers of the houses which were often hard to read. Porches were hooded, poorly lit. Meanwhile the minute hand on the dashboard moved into warp speed, malignant.

So far so good, she was gaining experience, but on her tenth night a headache slowed her down, neck aching from all the turns, the clutching, the brakes, the quick decisions. Streetcar tracks jolted her left and right. Someone thumped the passenger door with his fist and shouted. She drove on. Pepperoni and double cheese, this one. Construction on Bloor Street, a detour and then, believe it or not, at ten o'clock at night there was a marching band blocking the roadway. No way through the tubas, the snare drums, the top hats, the sparkling batons that the skinny white girls in skirts and stockings were twirling high into the night air.

Oh Jesus. She reversed the Kia, almost stalled, the car trembled and shook and jumped but she cut her way back through a fearsomely narrow alley and turned right. Wrong way, it was a one-way street. A ticket would finish her. But the clock said, okay, okay, still three minutes to spare. Couldn't see the house numbers though. She pulled into an open spot, got out, and started to run until there it was, number 37. Up the steps she hurdled, but the porch was full of cast-off boxes, cardboard, orange crates, two tricycles askew, a garbage can, piles of newspapers. A metal pipe or something caught her ankle. A jab of pain. She leaned for a second on a discarded barbecue tipped up against the front window. Heavy curtains, no lights on. She knocked on the door, the knocker a death's head, an iron skull with eye sockets shadowed, heavily ridged. Then she waited and listened and shouted, "Pizza! Pizza!" but her soft Spanish voice died at her feet.

Okay! She hammered *one-two-three-four* again with the knocker, put her ear to the door, bent down and flipped up the mail slot and peeked inside and saw a leg in blue jeans slide out of the way. "Pizza!" she shouted through the slot. Then the door was yanked open, and a hand grabbed the front of her coat and pulled her up and inside.

A large, bearded man, a dim vestibule.

"You're late with the pie. Oh, wait, hey, a girl! Well, this is something new. Something better."

He let go of her coat, but his hand moved down and touched her breast and stayed there. He pushed her against the closed door. With his other hand, he took the pizza box.

"Free, this pizza," he said.

A black T-shirt over muscles and belly and tattoos running wicked to both wrists. His hand where it was.

"You have made me wait at the door," said Estella.

"Knock, that's what the knocker's for. Now get out."

"The money, please."

Three more men came out in a phalanx from what might have been a kitchen. It was too dark to know.

"I was here on time, I knocked."

"You know what *fuck you* means? Stay another minute, you'll find out."

He opened the door and pushed her back onto the porch. "Thanks for the pie."

He slammed the door, the death's head jumped. She

looked at the mess on the porch for five seconds, walked back to the flickering roof light of the Kia, and drove away.

At 3 a.m. she told me how the bearded men had cheated her, how she'd been there on time even though the marching parade had slowed her down, how the first man waited to open the door then dragged her into the house, how he'd touched her on the breast and left his hand there, pushing her against the wall, how they threatened and said "fuck you," maybe she misunderstood, maybe "fuck" didn't always mean sex?

I said she hadn't misunderstood, I didn't think.

"Oh, Eduardo," she said, "it's more the money, the money we lost, after all that work."

I lay helplessly beside her. Over and over, I imagined the porch, the door, the hand. Then I asked her for the address of this house of cowards.

"No, I will not give you the address. They are too dangerous."

"We are Peruvians, we cannot accept this," I said.

"We need to be smart Peruvians. Revenge cannot be a reflex. We have no standing in this country."

I reminded her of what had happened years ago, how I had seen Vargas Llosa deliver a blow of revenge in defence of a woman. "Patricia," I had heard him say.

"Eduardo, you are not a violent man."

"The address, that's all I want."

"I tell you what we shall do," she said, "in the morning we will fill a wine bottle with gasoline. Then we will wait. If I am ever called again to deliver to that house, I promise, I will call you, Eduardo, and then you can be Mario Vargas Llosa, unchained. Just once, for us. If I am not called, then we will accept this as a learning experience. But we will not forget, we will not forever eat cake, I promise you."

No, she would not quit her job. Every other customer on every other night had been polite to her, and the tips more than covered the gas. She hadn't expected that. Once she was given a twenty-dollar bill, extra, on top of the usual.

So we settled into a routine. Friday and Saturday nights she drove Juan Antonio's Kia and in came thirty or forty or even fifty dollars. I found a job myself, a bit like in the library back in Lima, stacking shelves, but now it was with cans and packages of rice and tomatoes and soup and spaghetti. I began to speak English with ease, almost without thinking. Snow fell every day, then it was Christmas, then New Year's.

In January, at midnight, the phone rang. It was Estella from work, saying, "Eduardo? It's time. I'm supposed to go there again, to the house of the bearded men."

I checked the children. Sound sleepers, deep in their own worlds, far from ours.

From under the front porch, I extricated the gasoline-filled Rioja bottle we had sequestered out of sight, and I ran the five minutes to Clinton Street.

Already she had the pizza ready to go.

"Stay here," I said, "I will do this run."

"No, we are in this together. Here, the address, look."

"Let me drive."

Ten blocks away, we pulled up in front of the house. A parking spot was wide open, an omen of good fortune.

"Here it is, one free pizza," she said. "I have spelled out two of their words, *Fuck You*, on it, using pepperoni."

"Good," I said, "stay here and watch."

I was calm, under control. I knocked at the door and the death's head rattled up and down for me as it had for her, and one of the bearded men came to the door quickly, smiling, pointing to his watch.

"Late, goddammit."

I shrugged. "I know," I said. "What you get tonight is free, with our pleasure. I am sorry it has come to this."

I handed over the box and the door closed, and from within came male laughter receding decrescendo as they moved deeper into their lair.

It was far too dark on the porch for anyone on the street to see anything. Estella's face from the car window, a pale moon. I took the wine bottle from my jacket, unscrewed the top and opened the hatch of the ramshackle barbecue leaning against the front window.

Nasally, the sharp vapour of gasoline. "You will enjoy this vintage, it's Shell Regular and it goes well with pizza and cheese," I said.

I emptied it *trickling-trickling* into the black heart and belly of the beast. Streams of thin fluid ran invisibly, gurgling, overflowing, running down onto boxes and newspapers clumped below. Seeping to the semi-rotten floorboards that were sagging, creaking under my feet.

"Next, my friends!"

I cupped my hands, lit a cigarette, dropped it into the grill and walked briskly to the neighbours, first on one side, then the other. I hammered hard on their doors, a warning, but I didn't wait for anyone to answer. Then I walked back to the Kia and already there was a quiet but distinct crackling from the porch, an orange-red glow like an eye.

She was turned in the passenger seat, watching.

We drove around the block. We made it to the top of the one-way street in less than a minute, and there we waited, purposefully blocking the roadway. I checked my watch,

11:00. But the alarm was slow, 11:10 when the first siren came from the distance, and by then we were out of the car, standing like lovers between two darkened houses. The firetruck couldn't get past the Kia. The men jumped out, they leaned on the klaxon, pounded on the car. We ran out to them, I covering my face with my hands, waving as if to say "sorry, sorry," Estella close behind me.

I pulled the car up onto the sidewalk. The firemen blared past, one truck, two. Then I managed to park the car and together we ran down the street. By then there were other people running every which way, calling to their friends, and the house was already a bonfire gone halfway to hell. Firemen were everywhere. They'd jumped right off their trucks, but the flames were already porch to roof and licking from the upper windows. Neighbours on both sides had their garden hoses on full blast, doing the best they could, soaking down trees and bushes, the side walls of their houses. Then it got so hot they had to give up. They ran across the street and joined us.

"Christ, look at that," one of them said. He looked like a devil, his face lit by dancing flames.

Whoosh, the front window blew out. Glass shrapnelled into the yard with a wind-sucking roar. Tinder-dry for a hundred years, an inferno.

"Back door's nailed shut," shouted someone, "padlocked, iron grilles on the windows, the place is a fortress! Biker gang!"

Upstairs was the only place the men could go. Pitch-black was the smoke, crackling the flames. Coughing, wheezing, overweight, out-of-shape, in full-out panic mode the bikers must have clawed their way to the third floor because there they were, for all of us to see. Four of them, climbing one by one out of the high casement window. There wasn't much room on the ledge. They looked down, confused. Then they scrambled half-over each other up to the pitch of the roof.

The ladders were getting into position, stretching out, telescoping, but it was too late. The scorching heat, the toxic smear of gases. Desperate, all the pizza-eaters could do was jump, and so they did. Three of them, one by one, silhouetted against the raging orange and black of flames, and it was a long way down. They pinwheeled their arms, hitting the ground *thump-thump-thump*. The firemen were on them in a trice with oxygen, pulling them across the road into the relative cool, but there was little they could do. Covered them up quickly with tarps, then turned back and there was the fourth guy, crazy with fear, hanging from his fingers from the eaves. Then he too dropped, *whump*, right down onto the wrought-iron fence that ran between the houses. Spiked, skewered on it, chest and abdomen heaving, impaled. Another tarp was tented over him out of kindness, body hidden from view until the fire was more or less under control. Then the ambulance men were there, and with power tools they cut the whole section of fencing down, yanking him free, finally, like he was shish kebab.

The street, the sidewalks were awash with ice and slush. Water still arced high from multiple hoses, sizzling in the wreckage. Smoke drifted, a haze in the chill of the night. Charred remnants of the house lay jagged, a shell, smouldering.

Arm in arm, we watched as the firemen cleaned up, tilted back their hats, gathered by their trucks. I was trembling, seeing what we had done. "This is how he must have felt, Vargas Llosa, afterwards, shaking. Look at my hands."

"Adrenalin, Eduardo, it's a fighting hormone, it's natural."

"I don't feel good about this. Not entirely."

She stood on her toes and was just able to kiss me on the side of my neck. "I have been asleep too long, politically," she said.

A fireman asked us to step back as he rolled and coiled a hose in front of our feet.

"*Fuck you*, Eduardo, on that pizza, in English, is the

perfect slogan for predatory capitalism, for the system that creates uncaring men like that, heartless."

"I love you, Estella."

"This is the only violent political action we have ever undertaken, as a couple," she said, "and we have exceeded our wildest imaginings."

Before us lay a wasteland.

"We should get back to the children," I said.

There was not enough heat from the embers to warm us anymore. Two hoses played on, quietly shimmering. Grey ash had settled on top of the slush, a strange thick consistency under our feet.

"Rub your boots off like this, on the side of the curb," I said.

College Street was empty except for a taxi or two. No streetcars at this hour, the tracks of steel were glinting with cold. On Markham Street, a thin cat jumped through powdery snow and disappeared behind a garbage can. I pushed open the gate to our small front yard. With my foot, I adjusted the wooden lattice over the underside of the porch, where I had hidden the gasoline. All the houses on Markham Street, joined together in a long row, were dark.

I latched the gate and found the house key in my pocket.

"Eduardo, in the morning, I almost forgot, there's a

sale on light bulbs and various sundries at the big capitalist emporium."

"Honest Ed's?"

"Yes. It would be smart to be there early, before they open the doors."

We stayed up for a cup of tea, and we reached across the table to hold hands. Then we went to bed, and she folded the length of her body against mine as she fell asleep. Of course, it was still the deep darkness of winter, and the sun would not rise for hours.

Here in Canada, I have learned, there are animals called wolverines. They tread silently over crusts of snow. Their fur is pitch-black, yet they cannot be seen on the retina of the human eye. Like cobras in Peru, they have no pity on their prey. Pound for pound they are the quickest, most ferocious fighters in the world.

FIRST GIRLFRIEND

MOTHER WHIRLED AROUND and slammed the dining room door on Father's fingers. He groaned and fell to his knees.

"That'll teach you," she said.

A splotch of blood blossomed on the door jamb. My brothers and I exchanged glances. The cat crept in slow motion from the room.

Mother said, "Don't expect sympathy from me."

Father said, "Sorry, sorry."

"You should be," she said.

Then the doorbell rang, and I could see it was the paper girl, collecting.

"Not now!" shouted Father.

I had talked to her once at school, after we collided in the corridor. I'd apologized, she'd said okay.

"It's not her fault she showed up now," said Mother, "pay the girl."

Father called my name. I went to him and, from his crouched position, he handed me a five-dollar bill.

"There's blood on it," I said.

He waved me away. I opened the screen door and gave it to the paper girl.

"There's blood on this, fresh blood," she said.

"Check with the bank," I said, "I think it'll still work, come back if it doesn't."

Her two fingers were poised like tweezers, or pincers, stiffly, on one end of the money, avoiding the smear.

"Mine are separated," she said.

"Your fingers?" I asked, pointing to them.

"No, my parents, they had an irreconcilable difference. Three months ago."

We stood together, stock-still. The cat squeezed out between us and took off across the lawn in full-out run mode.

"Your dad should put bismuth powder on that cut," she said, "that's what mine used to do, it's an astringent."

Then there was a squeal of tires from the road, and a man jumped out of his car.

"Your cat," my first girlfriend said, "we better go check on your cat."

SWEET BOY

LEONA CALLED FROM THE AGENCY saying that an incredible opportunity had opened up, there could be no more procrastinating, and she kept repeating my name as she spoke—Timothy, Timothy—fearing my attention would slip, Mother watching me from across the kitchen, wiping the same sweep of counter five times, ten times—Leona, Leona, I echoed for reassurance—and so Leona continued, saying that Prince had called her, Prince the musician, his baritone voice unmistakable, asking her if she could recommend a young man to serve at his mansion in Chanhassen as a duster, someone skilled in the use of Swiffers, damp cloths, brooms, dustpans, ridiculous though it might seem, particles of dust were wreaking havoc on his creative process, and Leona did not hesitate or question him, instead she asked immediately if this would be a full-time position and he said yes, permanent and full time starting at twice the minimum wage but the job was no cakewalk, the household was imposing, 65,000 square feet, at which point Leona said, crossing her fingers, that she had the perfect candidate, Timothy Adams, nineteen, on self-imposed hiatus from the University of Minnesota despite a brilliant academic record, presently conflicted by an anxiety disorder but hard-working, honest, and she could have him at Prince's door at 7:30, just say the word, and rather than haggle Prince agreed, the arrangement was made, I was to report to Prince's mansion at 7:30 the next morning—Leona would text the details—and she reminded me that I would be representing the agency, that before meeting Prince I should familiarize myself with the passage from Genesis *for dust you are and to dust you shall return*, and although she was fond of me, all fondness had limits, she said, advice that I bashfully received, thanking her, hanging up, and there was Mother still polishing the counter clockwise, counter-clockwise, vigorously, and I told her that in the morning I would begin a promising position in the suburb of Chanhassen, dusting for Prince, at which news she dropped her cloth to the floor, pushed past me to the telephone and began to dial the number for our relatives in Lansing, cost be damned, but before that connection could be made I slipped away into the pantry, put on my winter coat and a pair of canvas gloves, and out I walked to the far meadow carrying a salt-lick for the deer, placing it upon a crust of frozen grass at the forest's edge, and then I stepped back and took a series of frosty breaths in the moonlight waiting for my friends to emerge, to abrade their tongues eagerly upon the blue-tinged surface as though salt were a drug rather than a physiological necessity, but the entire herd stayed in hiding, antlers indistinguishable from a myriad of inner branches, so I trudged homeward with mixed emotions, buoyed somewhat by my upcoming opportunity with Prince but chagrined still by unfocused melancholy, and next came a drawn-out whistle from a distant train, its mournful dirge torn ragged by winter's wind.

Next morning, my mother was a-bustle in the kitchen, bacon, eggs, buttered toast, "In the Hall of the Mountain King" blasting from the boombox, lunch in a paper bag, a kiss on the cheek, finally a friendly push into predawn Minnesota, and no doubt she watched as I walked the entire length of the driveway to the main road and disappeared behind a copse of cedar, then it was blacktop to the first stoplight where ice-fog blurred the semaphore of red-yellow-green, creating a dissociative atmosphere, I thought, but there was the proper bus, I climbed aboard and sat behind the driver and we arrived on schedule at the semi-rural suburb of Chanhassen, sun peeping up in the east like a yellow flare, and I was back on foot jittering my gloved hand against a chain-link fence up to an imposing gate controlled, I realized, by an electronic eye for it swung open at my shadow, its casters bumping over pellets of rock salt, and I became aware of a burly gateman saying Duster? and directing me toward a pearl-white mansion that appeared to be constructed from huge blocks of limestone, but in fact those blank walls turned out to be clad in a metallic shell of tempered steel or zinc, toward which I made my way as though at home with novel enterprise until I arrived at the threshold and an ordinary doorbell upon which I pressed, and *mirabile dictu*, Prince the musician himself swung open the massive door, first bowing to me respectfully then smiling, his expression entirely without the forbidding stare I associated, rightly or wrongly, with several of his album covers, and next he offered his hand to shake, and called me by my full name, Timothy Adams, standing aside for me to enter, taking my coat, laying it on a chair in the vestibule, holding me gently by the arm, taking me straight to the first doorway on our left into a small wainscoted chamber containing only a desk, a chair, and a standing lamp powered by a bulb of at least 200 watts,

I thought, for it cast palpable warmth as well as powerful illumination, and from the upper drawer of the desk he extracted a thin case of supple leather embossed at its edges in golden script, Arabic most likely, opening it gingerly, extracting a spectacular array of bespoke brushes, saying that these would be the primary tools of my trade, and he showed me how each brush was tipped by a single hair of sable or otter designed for a particular task, and then, tucking the leather case under his arm, he suggested we move on to what he called the Room of Blue Light, urging me to concentrate on landmarks as we moved along for he hoped I would become independent later in the day, an impossibility, I thought, for all I could see were closed doors and blank walls narrowing to perspective, such that Marco Polo himself would be lost without a compass, disorienting me at every step until we came to a full stop at what turned out to be an elevator flush with the wall on our left hand, its doors of brushed aluminum sliding open without a sound, and there we were, Prince and I, our reflections glancing off each other within the entirely mirrored interior, stopping me cold until I managed to focus on just one of his faces—I had five or six to choose from—and it struck me that Prince's public persona, his swagger, his brash confidence, might be a mask for public display, just as I wore a mask—though mine was far from his, mine was a mask of retreat, of abnegation—and that fugitive thought, that he and I could share a frailty, overwhelmed me, so much so that I put out a hand to support myself, but Prince quickly caught my wrist and guided me aboard, pointing out as the doors closed that the abundance of mirrors, their subtle angulations, were disconcerting at first but he had designed it so, to emphasize how fractured we were in self-concept, how universal was our desire to become whole, and that explanation so dovetailed with my own recent revelation—possibly we shared a frailty—that a calmness settled over me as I watched the flickering red numbers on the elevator's display drop from 3 to 2, earthward, the two of us disembarking to another empty corridor where Prince produced an iron key and unlocked the second door on our right, ushering us into a mid-size room with a vaulted ceiling from which cerulean light fell from an invisible source, cascading down upon a banked echelon of microphones—one hundred and five of them, Prince whispered—each nestled on bunched silk, and, after an appreciative pause, Prince chose two and placed them under a magnifying glass telescoping from the wall, and he showed me how intricate were the patterns of perforations, oval, round, square, rectangular, convex, concave, dead-flat, each according to purpose, whether for voice or instrument, and he pointed out that every single perforation harboured dust, usually in the form of a pearl-grey adhesive clump, and he worked with singular gusto upon three instruments, clearing microgranule after microgranule before saying it was my turn, handing me four microphones labelled A197 through A200, which I almost fumbled to the floor but Prince, as all good teachers must, pretended not to see, and an even greater calmness settled over me, along with a competence I had not felt for months, and we lost track of time together in the Room of Blue Light, I rapt by learning, he by mentoring, until he looked at his watch, groaned, stood up straight, apologized, and said that executives from the recording industry—devils incarnate—were expected upstairs but no worry, it was obvious that I had a natural, lovely gift of care and he had no qualms about leaving me, so I proceeded alone, skipping lunch—it was still in my coat's pocket upstairs—fastidiously cleaning the entire array of microphones, my speed and skill increasing exponentially as the hours passed until I fancied myself an accomplished duster adept at the detection and removal of all foreign substances, including specks of golden glitter fallen from the hair of singers, sticky granules of rosin from the bows of violins, dried spittle from explosive fricatives, trace deposits of facial powders for the hiding of blemishes, sugary distillates of whiskey mixed with exhalation-residues of nicotine and/or cannabis, and surely those were smears of cherry-red lipstick from whispering too closely or from spontaneous, uncontrollable bursts of laughter, to which go away! I whisked them with a dampened cloth, and as I relaxed into such an extraordinary new skill, time fled—my watch said 4 p.m.!—as from the corner of my eye I saw flakes of drywall cascading from cracks in the ceiling, dislodged, I realized, by heavy trucks rumbling on distant avenues, and I knew that my task would be circular in nature, it would never end, dust was dust, ubiquitous, a recognition that did not dismay me, quite the opposite, I stepped out from the Room of Blue Light intent on mastering the topography of the mansion, and what did I see but a ceaseless to-and-fro bustling from Prince's retinue, his housekeepers, cooks, and technicians, and I saw men and women leaning on walls, waiting to beseech him for advice or money, and in the vicinity of the recording studios I saw Prince's creative friends moving about and I knew, whether they were audio technicians, bassists, guitarists, videographers, film directors, drummers, dancers, all of them were unconsciously adding to Prince's burden with every gesture, and there and then I resolved to never let my employer down but to walk those halls every working day without mercy, pressing Swiffers against baseboards, windowsills, light switches, television screens, monitors, and I would scour the innermost recesses of closets and cupboards, a resolution I repeated to my mother that night over dinner, vowing that I would do those things for Prince, after all he had praised me in the presence of others and handed me an employee photo-tag and a key to the utilities closet, and although I knew Mother held greater hopes for me professionally, she was pleased and commented positively on the raised colour in my cheeks, the enthusiastic thrust of my day's report, and she said I obviously thrived when given responsibility and respect, and so I returned with a hop in my step on day two—the bus, the gate, the burly gateman—to find that Prince had left special orders extending my purlieu to his guitars, dozens of which hung on various walls by hooks and leather strappings, their electrical cords dangling to the floor, capturing semicircles of grit to be whisked away, and I saw without being told that each string of each guitar required cossetting with a semi-damp cloth, with the result that within a week I became known around the mansion as The Whirlwind, but truth be told Prince and I, The Whirlwind, never shared the intimacy of our first day together—in the Room of Blue Light—except for one singular time when I chanced upon him in Studio A, he sitting alone at the drum set unaware of my entrance, and it appeared that he was taking some medication for his hand was to his mouth, and next he swallowed water from a clear plastic bottle, and then he stood and turned in my direction, recognized me, fumbled a small container to the floor, and we both watched as several dozen oval tablets rolled and bounced in my direction, so that I scrambled for them—it being my job to do so—observing the numbers 10/325 stamped into each, Prince grimacing with pain. holding his hip, unable to join me in the hunt but thanking me—Timothy, Timothy—and he said that even three or four of those at once, Percocets, they were useless but what else could he do, and then he hobble-stepped out into the corridor and that was the last time I interacted with Prince other than receiving handwritten notes now and then praising me, such that I felt appreciated, and daily I approached the automatic gate to be recognized—Duster! Gateman!—as spring arrived to the whistles of cardinals, the burgeoning of catkins, the burgeoning too of money in my bank account for the first time, Mother and I agreeing that I had become at last a useful member of my demographic, until that horrible early morning of April 21 when Prince was found dead, slumped to the floor of his elevator, and I was terminated outside the mansion by one of his lawyers, checking my name on a clipboard, stroking me out with a black pen, sending me home as a nonentity, a fringe member within the bizarre entourage of the artist formerly known as Prince who, by his death, no longer held sway within his kingdom.

I returned home distraught, foregoing public transportation, walking for hours, and in the kitchen I turned the radio to NPR to hear commentators playing his music in memoriam, to rumours of drugs and private demons, and I reflected on how little we really knew each other, Prince and I, yet how generous he had been at a difficult time in my life, and when I heard Mother's car on the gravel I rushed out to the porch and shared the news with her and she cried for Prince, possibly for both of us as well, and afterwards we picked at a cold dinner until the sun began to set and I went to bed and slept fitfully and in the morning, surprisingly clear-headed, I phoned Leona and told her I was returning to school, that she could take me off the books, and Leona said that was the best news she'd heard in a long time, and she called me her sweet, sweet boy.

POLIO

IN 1953 THE POLIO VIRUS hovered over the summertime streets of Toronto. It multiplied in the warmth of slow-moving creeks and in the shallow sands of Ward's Island. In rainfall it slipped down from the canopy of maple, elm, heat, and cicadas, vaporizing into random bedrooms thought secure. It lay tasteless on the tongues of those who slept commingled there. Over breakfast we heard radio accounts of children slumped like rags, breathless, cyanotic, living out their lives within relentless metal carapaces, "iron lungs" pushing, pulling at the paralyzed chest itself incapable of moving air, and those children who had been rendered voiceless by tracheotomy used their teeth to go *click-click-click* drawing the attention of nurses to their plight (real or imagined), and the *click-click-clicking* ratcheted up as the sky darkened with ozone and thunder and the threat of power failure bringing parents, neighbours, and passersby unimpeded to the open wards in a rush of fear-of-smothering, the starch-white dresses of the nurses like moths amidst the to-and-fro swishing of tubes, the children lying as though beheaded, the sick quarantined, the healthy (you and I) taken to the cedar-filled air of Inverhuron, where the second of the Great Lakes beat against a series of reefs straight out from shore, where in the last shelf of rock—before the lake dropped off to what seemed to us to be fathoms of darkness—we could see the petrified coral bodies of tiny crustaceans, locked into their airless world centuries before polio.

ESTHER

LONG BEFORE WE WERE MARRIED, long before we had children, long before we assumed that kind of responsibility, we were given a rifle, a .303 Lee-Enfield, a relic of the Second World War, by a friend concerned for our safety, for it was our weekend habit then to hike the barrens north of Dawson City, where also lived the grizzly bear, eating voles and berries for the most part, we were told, but occasionally stretching his menu and his four-inch claws to humankind, if he were sufficiently irritated. But in fact nothing ever happened to cause either of us to raise that weapon, for *Ursus horribilis* never appeared before us personally, never huffed or gruffed at us, stalking only our imaginations on those high and lonesome hills where, it turned out, we walked in perfect safety for two years, the sun never setting in summer, sliding instead along the brow of the horizon only to rise up an hour later, and in wintertime there appeared, in the otherwise total darkness of the southern sky, just a glimmer, a pallor, a parody of daylight, during which all bears and carnivores but for Man hibernated, so in fact the danger to us, as hikers, was minimal, and we survived untorn-apart by predators, to then move back to Ontario, where we purchased a house on Suffolk Street, in Guelph, and there we wrapped our antique gun in burlap and hid it behind the furnace, breaking it down first into its constituent parts, its firing bolt removed and placed high in a closet, invisible, its five cartridges, rattling, sequestered in a small wooden box in a dresser drawer in our bedroom, thus rendering it ineffective for its deadly purpose.

Then we forgot about it. We married, and, as youth will naturally do, from that same bedroom one afternoon my wife walked, unbeknownst to her, in a pregnant state, and nine months later, well beknownst to her, she was in labour and delivered a baby whom we named Esther, and Esther was born with red hair, a surprise, for no one in our family had ever been born with red hair, and its presence demanded that we find adequate words to describe it, so we searched our common experience and said that it was as red as sumac in the fall, or like safflower, or like the ground-down red sandstone of Prince Edward

Island, upon which we had walked together when single, and those were the descriptives we used when speaking of Esther to friends who could not see her, to those who were blind, to those who lived far away, to whom we spoke only by telephone, and oh, how they responded with pleasure, universally, at hearing of her red hair, how they wanted to tell us their theories, that it was the result of a chromosomal twitch at the moment of conception, or a helical strand of DNA catching upon itself, or the transposition of a gene, or some other microcellular phenomenon that we could never fully grasp as laymen, but those speculations, however interesting, however well-intentioned, fell on deaf ears, for in fact my wife and I, as Esther's parents, had no desire to understand the colour of her hair, preferring it to be instead a mystery, or a miracle, as though, we imagined, we two were the planet Jupiter, deep in the Milky Way, and one morning we awoke to find a fifth Galilean moon circling us, a newcomer in our firmament, a heretofore unheard-of moon, a spectacular presence, yet we were content to be simply amazed at the new arrival, and did not seek to answer how, or why.

But it turned out that our preference for mystery was naive. It was not shared by others who, seeing the redness of Esther's hair—less red, they said, than lipstick, but redder than blush—could not simply celebrate it for what it was. There was instead a public thirst to find a reason, to account for it, and so, under mounting pressure, we had to say, eventually, to many of our acquaintances and neighbours, that no, my wife had not been unfaithful to me, and no, particularly no, our daughter's hair was not a Gift from Heaven as had been claimed by the dark-frocked gentleman across the street, a pastor of the Baptist church. His opinion we had to reject, for we were a secular family, skeptical of Gifts from Heaven, and skeptical too of the pastor himself for several reasons, the first being his constant affectation of certainty on matters of the heart—whereas we were uncertain of the same—and the second that despite his pale-stick softness of appearance, the pastor owned, paradoxically, a horizontally bristling Doberman pinscher, iron-collared, iron-chained, straining at his leash "most unlike a Christian," the pastor admitted, laughing, pulling back on the tether, "more like a heathen at the gates of Rome," scattering children and adults from the sidewalk twice daily, and leading us, as a couple, with our entirely dependent child in our stroller, to suspect, perhaps irrationally, perhaps not, the sincerity of the pastor's love for others, and the depth of his charity, which should, after all, have been his stock-in-trade as a pastor, and so we wondered if there might not be a different person lingering within the parson, so to speak, and, in fact, in light of those suspicions, we were frankly taken aback by his visit to our home upon our return from the hospital with Esther, when she was only three days old, when we heard a knock upon our door and there he was, hat in hand, wishing to see her, the baby, saying he had heard such wondrous reports, how intriguing the red of her hair, and whence came such a colour? and he handed us a gift just for her, a meticulously wrapped package of soaps and powders, and he gazed at her tenderly in her bassinet and touched her feet through the shawl with his fingertips, and spoke with a catch in his voice of her beauty—unformed, of course—how silken and how marvellous her hair, so similar in hue, he thought, to communion wine as used by Catholics and Anglicans, redder than the grape juice used by Baptists, certainly, and surely—what other explanation could there be—was that hair of hers not a direct Gift from Heaven? And no, no, he had no children of his own, no wife, no prospects either, too onerous were the responsibilities of a man of God, etc., etc., until finally, after the requisite cookies and tea, we ushered him out and wished him the best and watched him slip across the street, homeward bound, grateful that he was gone, grateful for the vanishing of the tension we felt in his presence, and I even wondered aloud then, to my wife, smiling, saying that perhaps his vestments were too tight to allow for procreation anyway, should he ever find a willing partner, an unchristian-like comment for me to make, but surely, we thought, he could not have heard us, for the front door had fully closed upon him before I spoke, and we returned then happily to gaze at our baby, at our little fifth moon of Jupiter, our new responsibility, and I waltzed her about the room to ease her crying, which had, we postulated, been precipitated by the pastor's lingering touch.

Several months passed in what was, but for lack of sleep, bliss for us. Then I realized, as a father must, that it was not enough to love our baby unconditionally, to bathe her and change her and pat her on the back, but I would also need to provide for her economically, that my non-existent earnings as a writer of verse would no longer suffice, adding as it did a supplement of zero to my wife's salary as a schoolteacher, so we decided that I should seek a wage-earning job outside my field of prosody and rhyme and, as it happened, I was in luck and soon was hired at the legal firm of Gatwick and Horton, on Woolwich Street, close to our home, where a bevy of lawyers worked at all facets of the law and required a factotum, a quick-footed run-about man, they said, to deliver files from desk to desk, to pour coffee for the partners, and then, as my talents became more widely known, to translate case files from English to French, and vice versa, gradually learning all the other sundry tricks of the paralegal trade, to which, surprisingly, I took with ease, so that within a year I could do a fully qualified lawyer's job but for their mandated appearances in court, and my services were provided at one-tenth their wage, a discrepancy I could not help but note, politically, as being the way of the world, but I held my tongue to meet the demands of our mortgage as Esther grew from toddler to child, and, in the passage of time, as they say, we provided for Esther two siblings, both boys, neither of whom had red hair.

It was then, after their births, that news came to us through the office grapevine that the pastor of the Baptist church had wondered aloud, at a social function, whether Esther's mother had not strayed from the marital bed when she produced their pretty little redhead, creating red from blond and from brown, a Mendelian impossibility, he had whispered to my confidante, who then related it to me, and, hearing such gossip reported, my wife and I decided that we should intervene and speak to the pastor, not vindictively but with kindness, for in fact for several years we had been troubled by his overly close attentions to Esther, how he seemed to watch her from his window, we thought, how he chanced to be on his porch whenever she played outside, riding her bicycle, tumbling on the grass, jumping at hopscotch, running aimlessly about, skipping rope, singing the child's rhythmic song "Jelly-on-the-Plate," or sitting curbside with her friends of similar age, ten or eleven, wearing their harmless shorts and T-shirts, harmless indeed, and perhaps, we thought, we had been too laissez-faire, too relaxed, too modern, too open, too understanding, allowing the pastor to pat our Esther on the head, to speak to her alone and at length on subjects as diverse, we discovered, as the baby Jesus and the colour of pollen and the song of the wood thrush, but how would we know what else he talked to her about?

Perhaps, we feared, we had allowed a wolf in sheep's clothing into our lives, a wolf crying softly *baa! baa!* and cropping at our grass, at Esther, our first child, while all we did was look away, or metaphorically pat that same wolf on the back and imagine a nice lady knitting woolly gloves from his soft and curling wool, off-white gloves to keep us warm in winter, and so we determined to go to the pastor and ask him, without casting direct aspersions, without suggesting impropriety where there had been none, to give our Esther space to breathe and grow, as we had learned to do as parents, to ask him to stop the flow of annual birthday cards, for example, each featuring, for some reason of his own, a new descriptive for her hair, ten adjectives over the years, words such as strawberry, vermilion, cardinalesque, auburn, powderyrouge, crimson, scarlet, fiery red, fugitive-red, glancing-red, and so on, so that we imagined him dipping into a thesaurus to write his cards, or into some outlandish lexicon of red, and, moreover, we would also ask him to cease accompanying each card with a present, be it a soft animal, an alphabet book, a music box, a doll, a battery-driven dog, a bible, a cylinder of Pick-Up Sticks, crayons, a copy of *The Wind in the Willows*, a ticket to accompany him to *The Nutcracker*, which event we actually allowed her to attend with him, as though to stamp with our approval their special relationship, and so it was then—when we first thought of him, possibly, as a wolf—that my wife said enough, enough, and took it upon herself to broach the subject with the pastor, for she was more adamant than I, I who thought only what a lonely man, and surely our imaginations were running amok around us, how crass we were, how suspicious, how Othello-like to imagine ill of a man of God, even going so far at my workplace, at Gatwick and Horton, to reassure myself by checking, via contacts at the police department, into the pastor's past, lest he be one of those tight-lipped clerics shuffled from place to place by bishops, by cardinals, by whatever superior ranks existed in his, the Baptist hierarchy.

I was assured by the police, in confidence, that he was a clean slate, a *tabula rasa* in the eyes of the judiciary, which put me somewhat at ease. Yet still my wife persisted, saying she would nip it in the bud, so to speak, whatever it was, even if it were the most innocent of flowers, a daisy or a buttercup, and not a Venus flytrap or a pitcher plant, and so she went to him, to his porch one spring morning, suggesting that Esther was old enough to no longer need cards and presents, that a smile, a wave would be enough for her, please, and he acquiesced, saying of course, of course, he wanted nothing but happiness for Esther, and so the cards and presents stopped, and Esther's birthdays went unrecognized except by her direct nuclear family, one birthday to the next until she was in high school excelling at mathematics, physics, track and field, and going to parties and dances, until, finally, as all children must, she left home, to Montreal, to McGill University, leaving her bedroom empty, from being just six pounds and sleeping in her crib to grown-and-gone in seventeen years, our Jupiter's fifth moon lost to our gravitational field, a sharp absence but one we had to accept, and would not have wanted otherwise, as parents.

A month later, after she left, an ambulance pulled up to the pastor's door. We stood watching in a low drizzle as a stretcher removed a fully covered body that could only be his, the attendants taking it carefully down the steps, sliding it behind the folding doors, and, without ceremony or siren, off the ambulance went to Norfolk Street, and at work that mid-morning, by celestial design or coincidence, I was asked to accompany one of our solicitors to the residence of a suicide, a single man, a pastor of the Baptist church, intestate, our job being to sort through his papers for signs of next of kin, to itemize his possessions, to secure the house against water and fire and leaking gas, and when we finished we were to lock the doors and leave, and oh, the solicitor said, there was a dog on the property as well, and so I found myself on my familiar street in an unfamiliar official capacity, taking the steps to the pastor's porch, to his door, to the wainscotting and the brocaded yellow curtains of his bachelor home, into which we had never been invited as neighbours, and as I entered his inner sanctum I did so with a tinge of sorrow, not so much for the pastor but for the transience of all our lives, thinking, however, that most of us would not leave by a violent gunshot to the head, which, we had been told, was the method used by the unfortunate man, the suicide, who must have ultimately found, my solicitor opined, his Faith insufficient, nor was there an explanatory note of any sort to help us at the scene, or to help the police in their investigation.

Those introspective thoughts of mine, upon opening the front door, were shattered immediately by a ferocious, guttural, non-stop thundering from the throat of the most recent Doberman, a younger dog, I thought, locked away in the cellar but mindlessly heaving himself against the intervening door, his claw-nails upon it like lashings of rain, destroying silence amidst the drifting of dust motes and the various parallelograms of sunlight cast upon the carpeted floors until, after ten minutes, during which we proceeded to the upstairs bedrooms and bathroom, all immaculate, the rage of the dog suddenly quieted by exhaustion, and we could hear our own breathing again, and we returned downstairs to the kitchen, upon whose linoleum floor we found a thick crusted bloodstain, partially oozed against the leg of a wooden chair, a testament to the violence inflicted, and I was then assigned, by my solicitor, to the pastor's desk in the front room, there to sit and examine his papers and put any pertinent financial records, if there were any, in my briefcase, and the rest I could do with what I liked, he said to me, for the pastor was gone and would not care.

It was then that my life as a parent was called directly into question because I found, within a minute, in the second drawer from the bottom, on the left, in its own small envelope, an initially upside-down photograph on which I saw the spidery letters V-I-X-E-N spelled in capitals, in red ink, and turning it over there was our Esther at eight years old, or nine years old, smiling, holding up a fish, a speckled trout or bass from, I thought, Lake Simcoe, her distinct halo of red hair encompassing not only the crown of her head but circling her face and touching her neck and shoulders, a photograph of an unguarded child tucked into the depths of the pastor's desk, with a difficult word, a suggestive word, written on its obverse, and I felt then as though my feet and my chair had become untethered from the floor, that I had no purchase of my own, that I was floating into the sunlight that poured over the roof of my own house, across the street, straight to the pastor's window, to that desk at which I sat transfixed but also in flux, my body floating yet my heart falling in my chest as sweat broke out to my face and hands as I searched for an innocent explanation for the photograph's presence in his desk, and not finding one, and then the solicitor called out to me with a question of no importance and the Doberman resumed his exertions against the door at the head of the stairs, shaking it just as my heart was shaking, until several more minutes passed and I was able to gather myself enough to say aloud that I was almost through, almost through, almost through at the pastor's desk, that I would be but a minute, simultaneously proceeding further, resigning myself to carry on, pushing myself, opening yet another of the tiny cubbyholes with a tiny key inserted to a tiny lock, a twist of my fingers, a *click*, and there I found, in that final secret place, against my will, for no reason I could comprehend, or ever wish to comprehend, Esther's ring from high school wrapped in a torn piece of ecumenical silk, silk as pale as Esther's skin, the ring tarnished for it was falsely gold, and then, tucked even deeper away I found a pair of her ankle socks with the initials E.R. sewn in cursive by my wife's own hand.

So I found myself in a nightmare as the animosity berserk in the living dog increased, rasping at me through the door, and then came the solicitor to my side, whistling tunelessly, and he said that we were through, we could leave the barking and madness behind, and he sighed and looked out the window and commented on the beauty of the highest trees, and I slipped the ring, the silk and the socks into my briefcase, and had I known the pastor well, my solicitor wanted to know, and I was able to say no, no, he was an enigma, the pastor, and back at the office I collected myself and searched out the police report, to which we had been given access for our morning's duties, describing how the pastor was found by the cleaning lady at 7:03 that morning, lifeless, lying atop a .303 Lee-Enfield rifle, serial number unknown to authorities, second finger still applied to the trigger, awkwardly, and awkward too was the firing angle achieved by such a long weapon, the officer thought, but there were no other signs of violence, nor was there forced entry to the household.

That night, after the two boys had gone to their bedrooms to read, to sleep, I went to our basement to check, for the first time in eighteen years, our rifle, given to us so many years ago in the Yukon Territory. But it was not there, it was gone from its hiding place, the burlap covering tossed to the floor, and gone too was the firing bolt from the high shelf in our closet, and gone were the five cartridges I had sequestered away as well, so it became clear to me then what had happened.

I came to my wife. I asked her to walk around the block with me, under our familiar trees haloed by streetlights, under vaults of chestnut, maple, beech, a dying elm or two, and I asked her how and when she had known, and she said that Esther had called home from Montreal, from a phone booth on Rue Sherbrooke, rue as in the English word *rue*, her voice as broken as glass, and then, my wife said, having suspected and disbelieved for too long, she had, upon comforting Esther, taken up the rifle and reconstituted it from its separate parts, and at midnight she had walked across the street to the Pastor's, to his back door, where she knocked, and the Pastor's face then appeared in the window and a bright light fell over her, bathing her as she was, resolute, holding the rifle at her side without apology, and she then watched as he took his dog by the collar and put him away in the basement, and then he opened the door to her, inviting her in, his body language surrendering, and he sat at the kitchen table with his head in his hands, as though he had been waiting for years.

By then we were walking arm in arm. We were almost home. I praised her for what she had done. We returned to our kitchen and sat together in companionship, waiting for what had to be said, for our own catharsis, and finally I reached for my briefcase and placed the photograph of Esther, her ring, her socks, upon the table, and we cried then for our daughter, the two of us sheltered within the intense umbrella of privacy that forms around all parents who cry for their children, impenetrable to others whatever the cause of their grief, and we openly questioned our past as parents, wondering where we had failed her, and how and why, failed to protect Esther despite the love we had for her, how we had walked her home from school, from music, to the library, to the pool at Lyon Park, to the market, our eyes upon her without fail until she was a teenager and downtown with friends, or canoeing at the lake, or doing any one of a thousand things she must have done, including, we remembered, those afternoons when the pastor called to her from his porch, saying, *"Esther! Esther!"* and off she went to sit with him out of kindness, we thought, and how stupid, how stupid we were, remembering how the pastor's Doberman dashed himself against the screen door, enraged, a centimetre, a thin aluminum screen away from tearing our daughter apart.

GEORGE MALLORY

ONE DAY, NEAR FIESOLE, friends drank and laughed and took nude photographs of George Mallory, saying forthrightly they could melt into his body. But evening fell and morning came and bells rang from the campanile. Flowers were strewn carelessly on linen, the party of paramours dispersed, and soon he, Mallory, was back in England and married, and forever after he carried his wife's picture in a small leather case looped by string around his neck as he set out for Nepal to climb Everest in the company of a close male friend. Together the two men stayed on Everest—inadvertently—for seventy-five years, until 1999, when Mallory was found by a search party, alone, on a sheer slant of rock and scree, a slope of thirty-five degrees, half-buried in candled ice, a torn segment of rope wrapped to his naked waist, face-down, smothered, chest scarified, arms held high, a sighing frozen butterfly bone-locked into black rock and dense shingle, scavenger-pocked at 27,000 feet, her image torn away from his chest.

But there was little time, the afternoon was falling away and the temperature too, a pallid sun was setting behind the North Col as these far-different men with oxygen, breath skewed only by altitude, took up their Leicas, their Nikons, dropped their gloves—red flowers tossed to hallowed ground—and, with fingers numb, snapped photographs again of this, their beloved Himalayan turned to porcelain.

THE PHOSPHORESCENCE

THE TWO MEN LEFT the apartment at 7 Rue Honoré Ugo just before sunrise, dressed identically in black shorts and muscle shirts, walking up the slight grade to the eastern end of Rue Rosetti to the gateway placed there by the City of Nice, the opening for which was cut into a stone wall topped with ornate and perforated wrought-iron in green and gold, reaching four metres high, and there they entered and headed upwards, beginning to run, shoulder to shoulder up the switchbacking staircase, taking turns to the inside, nine steps, nine steps, and so on, up and up into the semi-manicured pine forest of the "château" as it was called (though no château was there), up through dawn crickets and the slip of pine needles covering the upper reaches of the stairs until they came to the road that ran in from the north, and empty was the road in the expected coolness of the hour and now they were going faster, still breathing easily, until they reached the crown of the hill, a paved parking lot embellished by an irregular ring of low bushes, and on they ran, circling now for their return, settling into rhythm, past the lookout on the western precipice from which, had they stopped, they would have seen, beyond the darkness of the sea, the airport Côte d'Azur, its runway lights a-glitter, a low constellation flattened to the horizon, but they'd stopped for that view once the first time—three nights ago—so now they passed on, shoulder to shoulder, from the parking lot down to the forest, to the dawn crickets, the stairway, the gate, Rue Rosetti again, past stray cats shying away and cafés shuttered, running dead-centre now in the narrow streets and the half-blind alleys of the old city until they broke out into the Place Masséna, where black-and-white squares had been inlaid everywhere like giant chessboards geometrically conjoined, the squares of the chessboards a-blur at the pounding speed of their passing, to the Promenade des Anglais, where they turned westward, and already there was traffic, taxis, the first bus, and at last they stopped at the intersection of the Boulevard Gambetta and crossed to the seawall, looked down to the beach, their eyes accustomed to the dark and now, anyway, first light was glimmering in from the east, and there they saw the two girls, watched them as they came out of the water, swimming as early as the men had been running, returning to their bundled clothes or sleeping bags, lying down, somehow uncaught by the gendarmerie who swept the beaches till 3 a.m.—so, presumably, they had arrived after that—and the two men thought, wordlessly, simultaneously, that maybe these girls would do.

If so, it would save them a lot of trouble.

Shrugging, they crossed over to the Hotel Le Negresco, entered the lobby and made a phone call from the desk of the concierge, and then settled in to wait and within the hour the Caparellis were there, fully awake, walking into the lobby dressed to the nines as though they had never gone to bed, he with his hair punctiliously swept back and brilliantined, she in a kimono, flowered, immaculate, and immediately the four of them left the hotel, took the nearest steps to the beach, stood over the girls, who were fast asleep again in a tumble of sleeping bags and backpacks, and Sophia Caparelli bent down, her face lit by the rising sun, which was a limpid quarter-scarletine on the horizon, and she touched the bare shoulder of the nearer girl, gently, and said, in French, kindly, "Forgive me, but we are looking for someone, if possible, for the phosphorescence."

That's how the girls became involved, by falling asleep

on a beach and waking up. They weren't sure what the phosphorescence was but they'd seen signs on kiosks for it, posters in windows portraying a shower of golden stars, like fireworks, like Van Gogh's *Starry Night*, but they'd paid little attention at the time for they were hungry, they had very little money, they'd opted for a baguette and cheese and to sleep—the youth hostel having been closed at midnight—on the cobbled beach, because it was warm enough to do so, but now here they were, awoken still dazed within their sleepy heads by a woman kneeling down to them wearing a kimono, saying something to them, her lipsticked mouth as red as the early sun that hit her face slantwise, and with her were three men casting shadows, one white-suited with slicked-back hair, the other two in shorts and muscle shirts, hanging back respectfully, and the girls recognized something the woman was saying, the word "phosphorescence" in some strange accent of French, so they said first to each other and then to their new acquaintances "phosphorescence, okay," as if they knew, and the woman stood up and beckoned for them to come along, inviting them, switching to English, "everything is on the up-and-up," all they needed was two young girls with "courage and the right shape"—which must have meant stick-thin—because their two regulars, the woman said, "our Romanians," were held up at Ventimiglia with passport irregularities, yet the show must go on, the phosphorescence could hardly be postponed.

In a phalanx of six they crossed the Promenade des Anglais, waiting for the green light despite the sparse traffic of the hour, and as a group they entered the front door of "Le Negresco"—as the sign on the east facing proclaimed—and a far cry it was, this hotel, from the threadbare hostels of Cannes and Marseille. Pausing within, the man with slicked-back hair looked at them solicitously and asked, as though he already knew the answer, whether or not they had yet had their *petit-déjeuner*, and of course the answer to that was no, they'd barely woken up, so the men in muscle shirts sat aside incongruously in the lobby with magazines and pamphlets or tourist maps, waiting, while the girls were treated in the contiguous café to first a demitasse of coffee, dark and rich, then Belgian waffles heaped as thick as cobblestones, with strawberries, and for dessert they were offered and accepted apple tartes glistening with melted sugar, and a second tarte, this one of peach, equally sweet, following which the bill was paid with a quick signature ("You eat like little wolves," he said) and the floors over which they then walked to the elevator were made of highly polished marble or terrazzo, and in the mirrors flanking the elevator they saw their hair wild, thick a-tangle, a mad attractiveness they thought, wrought from benign neglect, and gilded were the accordion-like doors of the elevator closing upon them under the white-gloved hand of the attendant in his pressed suit of red with gold piping. They clattered upwards on invisible chains or ropes, pressed together in the confined and levitating space to floor *numéro six*, which, as they disembarked, was much simpler in decor than the lobby, plainer, utilitarian even, room 5 directly across from them just a few steps away as the white glove closed the latticed door, rattling, of the elevator, and the body of the attendant and then his head fell away as Kimono produced a key from under her loose garment and opened, with initial difficulty, door number 5, revealing a storeroom, its dust motes now disturbed, sucked up by the current of their entry from a floor of bare unpainted wood upon which a thick steel cable lay coiled, filling almost the entirety of the space to knee-level but for, against one wall, leaning haphazardly, three tattered papier-mâché constructions, bizarre and multicoloured in the rough shape of humans but with outsized heads. In the far wall was the only window, cut at shoulder-level, a narrow rectangular slit, the lower sill of which was blackened with the desiccated bodies of cluster flies. A desert odour of dryness, dust, and steel. Above them, presumably, the cupola, the dome of the Hotel Le Negresco, overlooking the bay, the crescent azure bay at Nice.

"Let's begin," the man said, and the strongmen bent to their task, found one end of the cable, snapped it to a ring provided in the stone wall, unlatched the dirt-encrusted window, levering it outwards as best they could until it complained, creaking with age, until its hinges of rust were bent outwards to an angle of forty-five degrees, and then slowly and with care they began to feed the wire—two centimetres in diameter—raising each coil which strained against its circular memory, feeding it through the narrow opening to the street below, and when their task was half-finished, the man with slicked-back hair turned to the waiting girls and asked them to remove their outer clothing, "Not everything, not everything, thank you," just their shorts and T-shirts, that they might put on instead the "costumes provided," formerly worn, he said with apparent regret, by "our two sweethearts now trapped at the border by government officials, cretins of conformity, no doubt," and the new girls did as they were asked and thus were standing in their underwear before the gaze of Kimono (the strongmen too busy to notice, their feet braced against the base of the wall, gloves of leather for the incremental slips in the cable as it fell away) and in turn the girls stepped, self-consciously, into the proffered one-piece swimsuits of blue silk, or perhaps faux-silk, identical, adorned by short golden knotted tassels falling from neckline and waist, marred by a few irregular spots of brown, possibly rust, staining the material in a pattern similar to that seen on the eggs of birds of prey. Then came "the harness, please," of which there were also two, taken from a worn valise in the corner, "wear it thusly, like so, around the waist, yes, and cinch it up, excuse me, here, between the legs, good, that's good, there," while the strongmen finished up, one of them clapping his hands in satisfaction as the interior cable now hung slack through the portal though much of its length still remained in the room, abutting their ankles and feet in such a way that they had to step gingerly, like gymnasts, but all present seemed satisfied as the girls' costumes were reappropriated, repacked into the one valise, and they put on their own clothes again—their prosaic bleached-by-summer wear—and they were back into the elevator, all six of them again, the troupe, down and out into the sun-provoked street where the cable now lay half on the road, half on the sidewalk, overseen there by two police cars pulled up at angles, squawk-boxes blaring, the avenue in both directions now closed to traffic, the strongmen beginning phase two, which was to half-roll, half-carry the widened coils, dull-silver now in reflected light filtering through the high palms, to pull them across the eerily stilled street, past the waiting cars, under the high globe lights that ran the length of the esplanade, ornate with curlicued standards, until, finally, here was the low railing that set the beach apart—the beach the girls had slept upon—small waves now making their uniform impressions on the shore with quiet regularity as the men took to a yellow rowboat waiting there, with thole pins instead of oarlocks, and therein and thereupon they loaded the rest of the cable, standing waist-deep in the water until, that task completed, they pulled themselves over the awkward tilt of the gunwales and, taking one oar each, rowed in synchrony straight out from shore, bending, rising, bending to their task, stopping only to ease the unravelling of the cord into the sea behind them until they came to a circular buoy of green glass, after the fashion of those used by Japanese fishermen whose nets and paraphernalia are torn by Pacific storms, and to this unusual buoy they made fast, then grasped the loose end of the cable and dove overboard, disappearing only to reappear and disappear again, attaching the cable end (the girls learned later) to a concrete mass in the shape of a battle rampart weighing eight tons on the floor of the sea complete with winch, electrified, which was now activated, and they watched, holding on to the side of the empty yellow boat now severely canted by their weight, as the cable slowly stretched itself and rose high, high, higher, from the seabed below to the tiny slit window above, on the sixth floor of the Hotel Le Negresco, taut as a violin string over a distance of at least two hundred metres, and the strongmen, now smiling, rowed back to shore while silent gulls wheeled overhead and they hauled the yellow boat above the mark for high tide, above the flotsam and jetsam and plastic bottles not yet picked up by patrols, coarse pebbles and stones turning under their feet as they pushed and pulled, and then they all walked together up the littoral to the railing, to the esplanade, the wire glistening high overhead, Kimono with her cherry mouth, her white skin, her formality, and by the stoplight the man with slicked-back hair produced fifty francs each for the girls, who then spent the afternoon resting under a rented umbrella, and, as arranged, in the evening they returned at nine to the Promenade, already jammed from the doors of the Hotel Le Negresco to the edge of the Mediterranean, five thousand onlookers, or ten thousand, several bands hammering away on drums and horns, coloured lights strung from the same ornate standards that had been cold and bare in the morning, lights circling around the sinuous trunks of the royal palms, and there was one of the strongmen wordlessly ushering them through the lobby, phalanxed together like starlets through a pushing crowd amidst the flash of lightbulbs, up the ratcheting elevator to storeroom number 5, where again they undressed, this time to nakedness, the putting-on of silk, the gold tassels, the leather harnesses snapped *click* first to their waists and then to new stainless-steel pulleys now suspended from the wire—two metres of which remained stretched inside, held fast by the imbedded ring—while from the street below came a booming of tympani, a rattle of snare drums in a descant of expectancy, and Kimono was there suddenly saying, "Remember, hold up your arms, hold up your arms and tuck your hair, like this," and "This is Vaseline I am putting here on the back of your neck, for protection," and thus the phosphorescence unfolded, as planned.

The first girl was lifted to the window (was that a pat on the back?), pretzelled herself through the opening and extended her arms in a V despite the chasm of uncertainty below, held fast where she was by the harnessed pulley overhead and by the strongman's hands upon her ankles while a weight, a backpack of some kind, was strapped fast to her shoulders, and the smell of butane or propane or alcohol touched her nostrils, then a cracking sound, a flash, and she felt the heat of flame and down she went, released in a feathering ball of fireworks of white, red, and gold, sparks shimmering from what appeared, from below, to be her wings, down and away, suspended from the wire, hurtling, the pulley hissing reptilian above her, and she felt the initial breath-sucking drop from gravity, then the slanting fall through the night palms, lights running up to her and brushing by, the beach below, the sea, the darkness, then cold, the sizzling of hot cordite as she hit the ocean hard, unprepared for this, stunned, and from shore the gathered thousands saw what they had come to see, the phosphorescence, phosphorescence charged from the impact zone, phosphorescence fused and lit in green and blue and red, an aurora pulsing, a trillion microplankton lit by the falling girl, who had herself been lit by fire, and the fire was contagious, it spread outwards unsmothered to the horizon, subaquatic, shimmering in a pulse undiminished while under the surface she couldn't breathe, the harness was pinning her to the cable, drowning her, she tried to rise, to swim until quick hands were upon her from behind and a mask of oxygen was clamped to her face and she was pulled up, up to the yellow boat, the surface, where now she hung by one arm, side by side with the second strongman, who said something to her in a language she didn't understand, his arm around her shoulders, and she watched what she had just done, her friend on her way down, the same V, the same fire, the fall, the boom of tympani, Hotel Le Negresco, the palms, the summer night, the invisible wire, the smash or crash landing three metres away and then the golden pulsing, the throbbing, the colour of the sea changing green to Africa, the phosphorescence for the thousands watching from shore, for the two girls from Savage Cove, Newfoundland, where beaches were too wild ever to be slept upon amidst squalls of rain, sleet, and snow from Labrador, from Greenland, where the St. Lawrence River blended seamlessly into the North Atlantic, the sun low at the zenith of wintertime, the pallid flickering-green from their own modest phosphorescence, rocks thrown three metres from shore, their life as it had been before this summer night in Nice, before they ran the wire.

Shaky, chilled, they were rowed back to shore forthwith by the strongman, who let go of the oars at the last instant, leaping from the prow into the shallows, surf breaking waist-high upon his back and legs, the grinding of wooden keel on stone amidst what was now pandemonium on the waterfront, the stretched-out arms of the gendarmerie cordoning off an area of perhaps thirty metres from the flash of cameras, from the pressing throng, from tympani, accordions, sirens, amplified voices booming down upon them as though it were a carnival—which it was, they realized, standing behind both strongmen now, just a few metres from the sea, uncertainly—the men shielding them physically from the gaze of the crowd, which by its insistence was growing closer to them despite the phalanx of officers, and, just as they had descended effortlessly down to the sea, along the wire, now, for the return journey, they were picked up suddenly in the arms of the strongmen, as effortlessly as though they were small children in their silk-and-tassels, hair unruly, soaked from a bath, backpacks of fire gone, stripped from them in the boat, and thus they were carried, the *phosphoresciennes*, as they were now called, apparently—*phosphoresciennes!*—by hundreds of voices, through hoarse clamour up the steps of the embankment, where white towelling was wrapped around them for warmth under the fin-de-siecle lamps of the Promenade, under the palms, straight through the front doors of the Hotel Le Negresco, which were held open for them by men in tunics of blue and red, faux-military, *ancien régime*, allowing them to enter the hotel while simultaneously, in the manner of those well-trained and practised, repulsing those not wanted from gaining ingress. Then Kimono was there, and the girls could stand on their own in the pale-white lobby, towels as soft carapaces, the monstrous chandelier of the Hotel Le Negresco golden-white above their heads, and cool was the floor of marble or terrazzo under their feet as the man with slicked-back hair and Kimono, the Caparellis, together, led the way to the elevator, a journey they had done twice already, earlier, but now surely this extraordinary experience was over, the strongmen were still in their shorts, shirts soaked tight to their chests, implacable, never meeting the eyes of the girls despite the close companionship, recently, the embraces under the shock of five metres of water, arms around each other's shoulders and waists, the classical position of lovers though they were not lovers, and up they went in the caged elevator to the sixth floor, to the life-sized humanoid broken sculptures, the rusted window, the cable still tight to the wall, straining, to their own street clothes placed neatly, cleaned and ironed though it was but twenty minutes (was that possible) since last they had been there, laid out upon two chairs, and Kimono told them to dress and the strongmen turned away while the Caparellis, less shy, watched them as they stripped their costumes to the floor and naked stepped back into the familiarity of their own clothing, bent to their running shoes. After which they were given an envelope of "some francs, for what you have donc for us" in the form of a thick packet bound in brown paper and pinched with elastic bands, criss-crossed, a packet that they were advised to place in the depths of one of their backpacks, "like so," the man with slicked-back hair said, "lest it be carelessly lost, but perhaps you are not altogether like our Romanians," and he went ahead to demonstrate his solicitude by placing the envelope himself, tucking it into one of the side pockets and closing the drawstrings, after which they were kissed on both cheeks by the Caparellis, man and wife, told they had done an "extraordinary job under difficult circumstances," that they had "matched our Romanians, wherever they are, in beauty and courage and, dare we say, bettered them in attitude," and "here are your sleeping bags"—giving one to each strongman to carry for them—and it was suggested that they leave the Hotel Le Negresco without delay, by the back door for if they were to venture out now upon the Promenade they would be quickly recognized, their photographs having been broadcast widely on television, their physical descriptions meticulously detailed on radio. In fact, now they were famous. They were the *phosphoresciennes*, and the reputation of paparazzi on the Riviera was well-earned, Sophia Caparelli said, as "feral dogs or jackals" wanting only to "chew and spit out" the lives of "mostly women" who had, by virtue of talent or beauty or inherited wealth, become celebrities, "however briefly."

Thus the girls left the Hotel Le Negresco through one of the back entrances, led by the strongmen through a door purposely built to be inconspicuous, and the street on which they found themselves was quiet, dark as befitted the hour, nor was this street illuminated by the otherwise-ubiquitous globe lights common to the city centre, and they were walking now along a seemingly endless fence of tall thin tightly spaced iron bars in black, tipped with spears of gold, going on forever, reaching nearly to the night sky as though cost were irrelevant, beyond which, through trees and parkland, they caught glimpses of a magnificent public building in ghostly white, ethereal, a building they could not identify for there were no signs for that purpose, and, turning right at the next intersection, they followed the east–west wall of black and golden spears toward, they understood, their destination, the youth hostel that had been closed to them the night before, and as they walked the environs began to assume the face of a normal city rather than a festive or regal one, with shuttered stores, dimly lit restaurants, streetfront patios, waiters busy or idle, bars from which shouts emerged, students or workmen going home, scooters, cyclists, cars idling half on the sidewalk, half off, and through this they weaved their way until—as a sign indicated—there they were at the Auberge Jeunesse Saint

Exupéry, on Rue Sacha Guitry, and the strongmen pushed open the heavy wooden door and spoke quickly to the concierge, who was, it appeared, no older than the girls and uninterested in their arrival, reading a book by André Gide, the title of which was not visible, the upper half of the cover of the paperback having been torn away. The young man finally said that perhaps they should take two beds on the girls-only side, for evidently they were girls and evidently "unaccompanied by friends of their own age," and one of the strongmen then suggested that the girls' backpacks be placed in a secure location under lock and key, to which the young man nodded assent and put down his book, reluctantly, took the backpacks and disappeared behind another door to emerge a few seconds later with a card that would give the girls access to their quarters anytime before midnight, after which the hostel would be closed, this hostel that has, he said, been named after a war hero, Saint Exupéry, yet is situated, ironically, on a street—Sacha Guitry—named for a Nazi collaborator, "Though what do you care about that," he said, "for you are all foreigners."

Then it was time, evidently, to say goodbye, and the two strongmen looked directly at the girls for the first time, at these *phosphoresciennes* whom several times in the course of duty they had held in their arms, saying goodbye to them, their accents from an eastern extreme of Europe, speaking nevertheless clearly but without emotion, their job finished. They turned and were gone and the young man at the desk, his Gide bookmarked by his fingers, raised his eyebrows to the girls as if to say, what could you be doing with men like that? and he proceeded to say out loud, "It's true that we are closed after midnight but if you're interested—a little secret—in one hour my friends and I will be going out to a club not far from here for dancing, and you are invited."

As they had let themselves be taken to the Hotel Le Negresco with little or no circumspection that morning, so an hour later the girls found themselves walking down narrow alleyways in what they were told was the old port area of the City of Nice (black was the darkness, street-lights broken, malfunctioning) to a cavernous warehouse where glitter lights rolled in the ceiling and strobes flashed ceaselessly and thousands were dancing rhythmically to music that slid through unfamiliar scales, the beat of drums African or Turkish or Azerbaijan, and they were handed drinks, "No alcohol, it's the truth, I promise!" by André Gide and his three friends, who were now giddy upon the dance floor, and despite the "no alcohol," after a second and third drink of the same, "Here, take this! Cold like strawberries!" they became dizzy as though drugged, they broke into sweats and fell into each other dancing while Gide and his friends laughed, wholly unconcerned over the girls' plight, girls frightened now as they had not been when they ran the wire to the sea, and desolation was their sudden visitor, a hollowness, an echoing within as, through the strobes and seizure-lights, they saw in the hands of André Gide a packet of brown paper criss-crossed with elastics, and he was throwing banknotes into the air, shouting *"les phosphoresciennes!"* pointing at them, and a thousand dancers then turned their way, coalescing like smoke, pushing them down a narrow corridor past washrooms, posters, EXIT / SORTIE signs in flashing pink neon until Gide was there again, saying "To the rescue! To the rescue!" apparently having the time of his life, joyous, shoving them through a doorway to a stifling closet so small they were unable to turn, jammed together. "There you go my darlings, soon we will return for an activity all girls enjoy, whether they are acrobats or not," an implicit and explicit threat, a *click* of a lock, but they were imbedded in that state of physical and psychological limbo for no more than a minute before they heard and felt, through the shoddy plaster surrounding them, an irregular series of rapid thuds similar to the sound made by sandbags thrown onto a wharf, and the door to their enclosure was ripped open not by Gide or his henchmen but by one of the strongmen, composed, relaxed within the splintered damage he had just created, offering both hands to the girls while his friend rose from the body of Gide splayed out against the floor and wall, and together the four of them left through the nearest EXIT / SORTIE calmly, wordlessly, hand in hand and hand in hand, first to a dank alleyway and then to the open street, to Rue du Lazaret, and a taxi.

Later the same night, an hour before sunrise, the strongmen left their apartment at 7 Rue Honoré Ugo and walked side by side up the gradual incline of Rue Rosetti, turning right through the same stone and wrought-iron gate as they had before, and they began to run up the switchbacked stairs into the semi-manicured woods, the dawn crickets, the parking lot hidden by low bushes, but this time they stopped purposefully at the western lookout, at the waist-high wall provided by the City of Nice, from which they could see the airport Cote d'Azur, from which by now the girls had already left for Paris, on Air France, and thence to Montreal. They stood for a minute, then down the hill they went shoulder to shoulder through the narrow streets and the half-blind alleys, Place Masséna, faster now along the Promenade des Anglais to the Hotel Le Negresco already returned to normalcy, stripped of its lights and music, of pomp and circumstance, and there they stopped and looked down to the beach, where there was no evidence now (but for the yellow boat) of the millimetre-deep flash of brilliance wrought by fire and chemistry, by living micro-plankton shuddering green and gold toward Africa, glowing so briefly in a layer no thicker than skin.

THE OXFORD BOOK OF MODERN VERSE

AT THE ABBEY THEATRE in Dublin, in 1934, Margot Ruddock came to the attention of William Butler Yeats. In a photograph, dark hair frames her face, a moonstone, her creamy pallor typical for Ireland back then, before Ryan Air, before the Riviera burnt winter away. An actress less than half his age, her voice was pitch-perfect for singing the old songs, for the recitation of poetry. He saw her first outside, leaning against a shadowed wall, backlit, a parenthesis. Inside, she sang and recited and he spoke to her, his incompetence with girls and women paring him away, saying, with your permission I could edit your verse. Oh, the flattering. She was bare to the world, undisguised by metaphor. Leaning toward her, over a small desk, light flickering, he said, I find rhythm wanting in your body of work. As if she didn't know it, as if she hadn't intended it, as though she hadn't reached out for the very lack of it. Married, a mother of two, a skewed gyroscope, her chameleon moods. Finally he succumbed to her, a touch on her shoulder, unbuttoning her in Donegal in November, the hotel under direct assault by a north wind that had driven even the sheep indoors. He recovered his potency with her, a Second Coming, and in good faith he included seven of her poems in *The Oxford Book of Modern Verse*, 1936. Then he went to Spain with his wife to translate the Upanishads, Margot's pulse still beating in his head, her white skin addictive, her body a nightmare, a train wreck, brakes shot on the narrow-gauge, drive-wheel spinning, other passengers jumping for their lives while he stayed off-balance, shovelling coal into her, and the heat of her body burnt holes in his hands and his face and his falling-down gabardine trousers, dawn finally breaking to the soporific breezes of Palma, Majorca. The morning post, her letters on a silver tray unanswered. Then Barcelona, where she cleaved and broke, alone in the Plaza de Colom, her only friends dogs and vagrants and midnight vendors of street food, cobblestones, her own footsteps leading up a staircase to an anonymous roof, to a skylight in a green and rusty metal frame down through which she fell—not as you or I would fall, thinking *oh no oh no*—with no thought in her head at all, down through shards of glass to an earthen floor where three Catalans, surprised, used everything at hand to staunch the blood that flowed from her glittering veins, restaurant linen, aprons stained with the juice of beets, prunes, mustard, the sauce of soups and apples, daubing and pressing until they ran to the street and waved down the Guàrdia Urbana and the Guàrdia Urbana carried her away. Next she entered a series of hospitals from which she never recovered, and in our world today, 2025, no mention is made of her, of Margot Ruddock, nor is she included in *The Oxford Book of Modern Verse*, but the wild swans at Coole still turn their heads to look, and falcons twist against leather restraints, and the bishops of Ireland remain as mute as ever to the sounds the wounded make.

VENTIMIGLIA

THE TWO STRONGMEN SET out twenty minutes before dawn, stepping down from their caravan, weaving between horses, between cooking fires smouldering from the night before, past sleeping elephants, cages of large cats curtained against disturbance, the bear in his wagon shifting his weight, various serpents lolling from trees, Peruvian fruit bats ghosting after insects, foxes and dogs huddled on burlap, odours of tangerine, curry, dust, grape, tomato, dung, urine, feeling their way through darkness until they reached the open scrub that dominated the hills above Ventimiglia. There starlight allowed them to see their footing. They began to run, shoulder to shoulder down tight switchbacks, keeping to the centre of the narrow road, crumbling rockface or walls of meticulous stone holding back the hillside from erosion. Finally the angle of descent eased and they crossed over railroad tracks to the Genoa road, the first hint of daylight casting its panhistorical glance over the amphitheatre the Romans left behind, half-fallen to rubble. No matter, they passed it by, picking up the pace, breathing easily, turning left at Via Cornelio Tacito, matching stride for stride to the seawall where feathered palms rustled in the wind and small waves curled, white on black. Passeggiata Trento e Trieste, prosaic apartments lining its landward side, shuttered cafés, intermittent orbs of light from Art Deco lamps, swan-necked, twin-flowered, falling upon their shoulders as they passed underneath, their shadows criss-crossing, blending, disappearing. The road changed its name. It turned to the north. They ran beside the palisaded fence of the public gardens, gates locked against intrusion. At the first roundabout they slowed to half pace and right-angled into a warren of narrower streets. Outside number 12, Via Aprosio, they stopped. Theatrically, the morning's first ray of sunlight then broke over the rooftops, spotlighting the sign that hung over their heads, *Polizia di Stato*—state police. As though professionally stage-managed, the Caparellis immediately rounded the corner from Via Bligny, Raffaele as punctilious as ever in his white suit, his dark hair swept back, brilliantined, and she, Sophia, wearing a flowered kimono, one velvet-slippered foot in green, the other in gold. The two strongmen, by contrast, were plainly dressed in black shorts and T-shirts, to which circles of sweat had accrued in the last half-hour.

The Caparellis did not have to break stride. The strongmen opened the door to the station. As a group they entered a large waiting room, poorly lit by wall sconces. There was a stationary ceiling fan, three wooden benches to one side, a wire ceiling-to-floor partition through which an opening had been cut at shoulder height for the duty officer. He, a young man, acknowledged them by jumping to his feet and saying, "Ah, the Caparellis." He left his post, beckoned for them to follow, led them down a corridor to a room that said, on its door, *Sala Conferenze*. "How rare it is," the policeman said, "for the captain to appear at this hour." He offered them seats at a much-worn table. He pulled out several chairs. Sepia photographs of Ventimiglia—the seashore, the Basilica, the bridge over the river—sat slightly askew on the walls. Then he left, but even as he retreated a new and heavier set of footsteps approached, and the portly Captain Albertini—so read his name tag—clean-shaven, in full uniform, rushed into the room.

"Gentlemen!" he said, "and Signora, a pleasure!"

He shook hands with the Caparellis. He nodded to the strongmen. He gestured to the chairs, they sat informally, wherever they wished. He removed his hat, leaned forward and said, "Thirty years in Ventimiglia, for the Balcescu Circus! Who would believe it? Yet, after all that history, I understand there is an issue."

"Indeed, Captain," said Sophia, "but nothing insurmountable."

"Proceed then, Signora."

"Since 1953, Captain, we have been granted, by the City of Ventimiglia, permission to bathe our animals in the sea. This arrangement, this courtesy, was hammered out by my father with one of your predecessors, yet here we are, day three since our arrival, and the permit has not arrived. Moreover, a concrete barrier has been inserted into the seawall at the foot of Via Cornelio Tacito, blocking the entrance to our traditional beach. However, even more importantly, there is the issue of our Romanian girls, our finest aerialists, presently being held here under lock and key. They have committed no crime. They are vital to our success in France. We demand their release."

"Signora," said the captain, "a touchy situation, yes. Consider my position. Our mayor came to me yesterday, complaining that the Balcescu Circus uses Ventimiglia as a staging ground. You bathe your animals, yes, but we receive little benefit. None actually. In fact, my mayor says, many of your larger beasts—it is not their fault, it is natural—are so encrusted in filth, dung even, that our shoreline requires scrubbing afterwards. Perhaps he exaggerates. But, Signora Caparelli, the mayor shows me photographs of French beaches contaminated only by the sheen of sunblock and the bodies of starlets. In Nice, he tells me, your pretty little Romanians attract a crowd of ten thousand paying customers. Thirty thousand francs pour into the municipal coffers. Your girls, we are told, are somehow set aflame at midnight, cast out upon a wire from the rooftop of the Hotel Le Negresco, sent at dizzying speed over the Promenade, the stately palms, the cobbled beach. They sizzle into the sea, the sea catches fire, it shimmers in green all the way to Morocco. Ten thousand paying customers are left breathless. A circus trick, of course, but however it is done—and this is the point, Signora—we in Ventimiglia will never see it. Your little fireballs will never perform here, for us. Instead, we see the washing of the animals."

"Captain," said Sophia Capparelli, "to be blunt, your waterfront lacks the necessary architectural splendour. Technically, with concrete reinforcements, we could perhaps use one of the towers in the old city as a launching pad, but the distance is too great. Our aerialists would burn to a crisp. And forgive me, for a sensitive man you sell short the beauty of the washing of the animals. It is a dignified ceremony, untainted by artifice."

"It does have its charms," said the captain, "that I admit."

"We are pleased to offer a considerable sum of money for the scrubbing of your shoreline, afterwards," said Raffaele Capparelli.

He handed an envelope across the table. The captain, after checking its thickness between thumb and fingers, tucked it into his pocket. "The sergeant," he said, "at the desk, will have your permit. But your Romanians are a different matter. Passport irregularities cannot be overlooked. Their documents are suspicious, to say the least. For goodness sake, Signora, they have exactly the same photograph."

"They are identical twins," said Sophia Capparelli.

"And they have exactly the same impossible name," said the captain. He consulted a piece of paper he had sequestered in his hat. "Katia Elena Cristina Petronela Vladimirescu."

"A parent's prerogative, in Romania, for the naming of twins."

"Since their apprehension, they have treated us with disdain. They have no respect for authority. If privileges are denied, or even delayed, they have tempers."

"They came to us as teenagers, much abused."

"Regardless, Signora, believe me, there is nothing I can do. Their papers are on the way to Rome. The matter is out of my hands."

"They are prone to asthma, Captain, if confined to damp quarters."

"Our cells are in the basement, but there are high windows. They are well cared for."

The Caparellis and the strongmen stood to their feet. They thanked the captain. Outside they stood together amidst the clattering-open of shutters, carts with produce weaving by. "Okay," said Sophia Caparelli, "if that's the extent of their cooperation, circle the building, find out where they are, we'll leave with them directly from the beach."

The station covered an entire block, its ground-level windows opaque, of thick frosted glass bolstered on the outside by vertical iron bars. The strongmen began to walk the entire circuit, whistling like warblers, tunefully, but it wasn't until they had reached the west end of Via Bligny that they heard a reply, an owl's low hooting. Then laughter, another hoot, then an overly ecstatic chorus of warblers. The strongmen tapped on the window twice. Then they began to run again, but no longer side by side, forging their way through increasing traffic back to the Genoa road, the amphitheatre, the railway, the hill, the switchbacks, the circus awakening, cooking fires ablaze, thirty men and women crouched over breakfast, the bells of harness and tack ringing through the grove of lemon trees.

They clapped their hands. Within an hour the trek to the sea had begun. The seven African elephants took the lead, stepping carefully down the incline, daintily, unused to such heights, followed by an extended train of horse-drawn red and yellow caravans bending themselves around corners so tight that wooden brakes rubbed on wood, iron on iron. Yet somehow those dozens of turns were made without incident. Down the steep hill came the entire belongings of the Balcescu Circus, four large tents, a thousand metres of rope, the platform for the trapeze, high-wires tightly coiled, assorted wrenches for tightening, the carousel in thirty-seven sections secured by clamps, star-topped kiosks for tickets and promotion, costumes for those who swallowed swords and breathed fire, the crystal ball, the ringmaster's hat, his tuxedo and shoes, barbells real and counterfeit, decks of tarot cards, thousands of such items brought to sea level by slow and dignified parade. To the Genoa road, to Via Cornelio Tacito. Arriving at the seawall, they found the concrete barrier shunted aside. The first elephant stepped down to the beach unimpeded. She hurried to the ocean, bent her knees, threw her trunk in the air. Then followed six of her brothers and sisters in an equal rush, stamping their feet into the breaking waves. Water flew in all directions. Then came, either free or on leashes, three tigers, the Alaskan bear, two camels, a dromedary, the lone zebra, a dozen seals free to do whatever they pleased, the waddling sea lion, a slow tortoise, workhorses released from duties, ponies with coloured tassels in their manes. A shrill whistle sounded. The washing of the animals began in earnest. The three elephant trainers, the ringmaster in his underwear, four equestrians in red tunics, the aerialists—but for the Romanians—wearing glittering tights of blue and gold, six clowns in uniform, dozens who cooked and cleaned, welded and hammered, electricians and scene painters in various stages of undress, all armed themselves with long-handled brushes or mops. The Siamese twins, the Wolf Boy, the tattooed sailor, the fortune teller, the dwarf with his monkey, those who sold tickets, those who spun candy, those who played the accordion and the calliope, all took to the ocean in a grand frenzy, a mad yet organized splashing, reaching for and scrubbing the flanks of the nearest animal. Nor were they averse to playfully poking and knocking each other topsy-turvy in the surf. Nor did the children of Ventimiglia hesitate to join them, darting about in ecstasy, resilient to collision, falling underwater, rising again. Overhead, to complete the visual and auditory mayhem, raucous squadrons of gulls flew furious at the morning's unexpected delirium, forced to share the air with parrots and cockatoos, falcons released from blindfolds and perches, one dignified albatross, forty mad-dash puffins, the rooster who could count to thirty-five. Leaning on the seawall was the captain of the state police, and beside him was the mayor, wearing his official chain of office, shaking his head, both too enthralled to notice that the strongmen had disappeared.

And where were they? Half an hour ago they separated themselves from the ceremony. Their caravan clip-clopped unhurriedly along the waterfront and turned north at the river. At the corner of Via Bligny, at the police station, at the predetermined window, they brought their horse to a halt. They whistled for reassurance and the owls answered. Standing together on the roof of the caravan, they reached upwards and taped the edge of a drop-sheet to the closest window ledge. They unfurled it to the sidewalk. Passersby could then see a prancing white unicorn rampant upon a field of forget-me-nots. The citizens were captivated. They stopped to watch as the second strongman set up as a busker, playing an accomplished fiddle, open case at his feet. Meanwhile his partner in justified crime slipped behind the curtain, reached through the bars with a glass cutter and expertly, using suction cups for control, cut a perfect rectangle from the windowpane. One metre high, fourteen centimetres wide. He pulled it free and set it against the wall, and then he took a silken rope from his pocket, dropped its knotted end into the cell below, waited a moment, pulled up the first Katia, the second Katia. Dark eyes, dark hair, they were just children, waifs, far too fragile for imprisonment. Like cats they squeezed easily between the bars. Expressing no gratitude, they watched as the strongman taped the window back into place, and then all three slid out against the wall into bright sunshine. The girls bent and stretched and leapt of their own volition through the open door of the caravan. There they curled up in each other's arms, resting on a narrow couch, on leopard-skins thrown there for comfort, and they closed their eyes, as though their days in custody had been spent, despite their recent laughter, on high alert.

The strongmen took up the reins. They began the four-hour journey to France, crossing the main bridge, passing below the old city, skirting the harbour, making their way up into the hills under mottled shade of cypress and plane. Cars passed continuously, deferentially, drivers and passengers waving, enchanted. By noon, relaxed in self-reverie, speaking little, they passed the Hanbury Gardens. Approaching the border, they avoided the tunnel on behalf of their horse's known preference for daylight, keeping to the upper road, going downhill past flowering walls of bougainvillea, towering cliffs, the glittering sea. Within view of France, its flag, the low building of the Sûreté Nationale, they came to a lay-by. There they should wait, they thought, for the others.

Two minutes later, the Caparellis' red Fiat swung past them and stopped on the shoulder of the road. An interweaving chorus of sirens was not far behind. Two police cars, possibly overexposed to American cinema, sped down upon them, braking, skidding, sliding dangerously close to the horse in his traces, blocking the roadway. Captain Albertini launched himself from the lead vehicle, snapping his fingers, saying, "The key, the key, the key, please."

The strongmen felt the caravan begin to shake beneath them. They heard a low growling, a snarling. "Exercise caution," they wanted to say, but the captain had already spotted the skeleton key hanging on a nail by the door. He grabbed it eagerly, fumbled it to the ground, picked it up, and he was about to reach for the lock when the door splintered outwardly and a single leopard's paw, yellow, rosetted in black, claws extended, twisted its way through the wood, through red and yellow paint, seeking a target, catching the captain by the sleeve, swiping downwards, shredding the material.

"Madonna santa!" the captain cried. He fell back. His bare arm was unbloodied, untouched. The paw retracted. A junior policeman drew his pistol. The strongmen in unison jumped down from their seat and blocked the line of fire. "No," they said, aware of the delicacy of the situation, aware that bruised authority might strike for no reason. They looked for Sophia Capparelli, and she did not disappoint them. She arose from the passenger seat of the Fiat, kimonoed, and all eyes fell upon her, from the policemen, from a gathering crowd of motorists unable to pass. She gestured for the pistol to be lowered, and was obeyed. She inspected the captain's arm, which he allowed her to do. She walked to the caravan's door, pulled it open—it had never been locked—and then she stood back as two young leopards jumped out, carefree, relaxed, yawning. They rubbed up against her. She looped a leash around each of their necks. Like mirror images, they sat on either side of her. "Note their composure, superior to ours," she said. Applause broke out from the onlookers. It was twenty years since the strongmen had seen her in her original role. She

made one minor adjustment to her posture, tucking the heel of her right foot into the instep of the left.

The captain bowed to her. He walked to the caravan and looked inside. "Impressive, Signora. Next year in Ventimiglia, we shall double our vigilance and triple our fee for damaged property." He held up his arm, his torn sleeve. Raffaele Capparelli stepped forward with an envelope. Two minutes later the police cars had turned about in the roadway and, at modest speed, disappeared to the south. Traffic resumed in both directions.

"I hope they will be ready for Nice, the girls," Raffaele said.

"They are young, not fully trained, it will take them several days. We need to seek alternatives," Sophia said. She ruffled their ears.

The offshore breeze was picking up, dropping down from the white cliffs, snapping at the French and Italian flags, blowing grit from the roads, scouring the beaches, flattening the waves on their way to shore. The leopards lay down on the shoulder of the road, on gravel. The strongmen and the Caparellis leaned against the Fiat. Already they could hear, despite the distance, the travelling bells of the main body of the Balcescu Circus, charming, magical, coming their way.

TRANSFORMATION

IN 1611 HENRY HUDSON was set adrift by mutineers, put over the side of the *Discovery* into a small boat, vilified, tumbled against the gunwales, gaffed away with his son and seven other sailors loyal to him from the lee side of the mother ship into the open, pitching, vast northern ocean we now know as Hudson Bay, a dreary seascape of wave-chop and tidal wash, shoreline of tundra and muskeg semi-suffused by static light and little sound, as though the sun were in partial eclipse, as though there were no birds, or birds had no voice, and historians tell us that these castaways were never heard from again, that Hudson had no sextant, that they drowned, but that was the opinion of Europeans who did not take into account the appearance in Inuit legend of a wooden boat with oars driven by relentless winds onto the sandbars far east of what is now Qamani'tuaq, a white man and a boy together wading ashore in the thinnest of shirts, lying down on ground inhospitable for 343 years until the northern hemisphere turned their bones to chalk, until their shoulders bristled through ragged linen and they rose again into the crystal night of winter and walked as caribou into the year 1954, when three Inuit hunters, starving, rested their army-surplus .303s on shoreline hummocks and shot so simultaneously that only one echo was heard, and amidst the blood congealing there they assembled their cutting tools, shook the animals' hooves in greeting, cut their tendons ceremoniously, took snow into their mouths and pressed their lips, trembling—they were teenagers—to the still-warm lips of the English sailors dead from the south.

THE LUXEMBOURG GARDENS

IN SEPTEMBER OF 1961, when I was sixteen, I flew to Paris. I was to stay with a French family on the first leg of a student exchange. But things got mixed up in a hurry. The family's grandmother, in Marseille, suffered a series of strokes, causing the mother and father to rush off together to care for an extensive property. The two daughters went with them, so I was left with just my new friend, their son Pascal, at their apartment on Rue Budé, on the Île St. Louis. Then, within a week, Pascal was arrested for, of all things, sedition. He was involved with a radical student organization, or "cell" as it was characterized in *Le Monde*, dedicated to the realization of self-government for France's closest possession, Algeria. Bail was out of the question. All France was spooked by the fear of insurgency. After an hour of struggling with long-distance codes, I managed to contact the father in Marseille with the news, but no, he would not return. "Pascal has made his bed with Communists. He will suffer the consequences." The father apologized for deserting me but said that if I walked daily across the Pont St. Michel, if I purchased a baguette and cheese and then walked for two hours in any one of the twelve directions of the clock, if I spoke openly to passersby, my vocabulary would improve and my life would be enriched. "I have told Pascal the same, but he is oblivious to common sense. You shall do better." We were speaking in French, of course. He instructed me on watering his plants. "Thank you," I said.

I hung up, feeling disheartened. Who could have imagined this? I thought of phoning home, but the complexity and the cost were overwhelming. I was on my own. Locking up the apartment, I descended three flights of stairs to the inner courtyard, looking up at jury-rigged laundry lines suspended from various windows. I waved *au revoir* to the elderly concierge and pushed open the heavy door to the city. I would follow instructions, I would enrich my life. To that end I crossed the nearest bridge to the cathedral, raised my eyes to examine the gargoyles—I had no idea of their meaning or import—and then, map in hand, set out in a northerly direction, imagining the hand of a clock pointing to noon.

I first crossed the river, or a branch of it, on the Pont d'Arcole. Soon I found myself in a large public square, and after that the roads narrowed and became more commercial. I passed pastry shops, flower shops. At a boulangerie I purchased, as per my instructions, a half-baguette with cheese and sliced tomatoes, wrapped tightly in white paper. But I was too nervous to eat it on the spot, and there were no benches or green spaces. On I walked, without direct purpose, my sandwich pinched between arm and chest, leaving my hands free for the map. It quickly became clear that Pascal's father's advice, to walk in a straight direction, was impractical. Narrow streets branched off at differing angles, drawing me irresistibly off course. I attempted to make corrections, but after an hour or so of indecision I found myself at the foot of a funicular, a short tramline that rose, my map indicated, from Place St. Pierre to the Basilica du Sacré-Coeur. I had wandered perhaps a quarter mile from my intended path. Still, not bad, I thought, for my first day.

The fare for the funicular was not exorbitant, but as my funds were limited, I took the adjacent stairway up through steep parkland, arriving at the top in a well-earned sweat. There I leaned on the ornamental balustrade that overlooked the city. I could not see the river, nor the steeples of

Notre-Dame. Feeling hungry at last, I placed my sandwich on the parapet and unwrapped it, but the brie, or camembert, or whatever cheese it was, had melted during my journey. It was oozing from between the cut edges of the baguette, along with juice from the tomatoes. Quickly I replaced it on the parapet, intending to search my pockets for a napkin or handkerchief. Before I could say "Hey!" or "Zut alors!" a wolf-like dog came out of nowhere, sickly yellow in colour, collarless, bristling. He snatched my meal between his jaws and raced away through a crowd of onlookers. Laughter ensued. I smiled as though equally amused, noticing for the first time how olive-skinned or sunburnt were the faces about me. Perhaps there was an African or Algerian quarter in Paris, and I had stumbled into it.

An elderly lady then approached me, dressed in widow's black. She was carrying a small tray and offered me, in sympathy, a slice of pizza. I was touched by her kindness, but the main ingredient appeared to be green olives. Therefore I shook my head, but she insisted, holding a piece up to my face, almost pushing it into my mouth. Well, go ahead, I thought, so I took a bite from it. "Very good," I said, pretending satisfaction, but it was salty to the extreme. She then rubbed her fingers together and produced, with one dexterous hand, from a pocket in her dress, a handwritten bill for five francs. "For me?" I asked. "For that slice of excellent pizza, of course," she said, and so I spent one-half of my daily walk-about money for a salty tongue. I counted out the coins, one by one.

Then I broke free of the gathered crowd, all of whom were openly enjoying my discomfort, smiling, laughing, clapping each other on the back. To escape, I set out to circumnavigate the Basilica. There was a charge for visiting its dome—curiously Turkish in design, I thought—but circumstances worked in my favour. I was swept up in a crowd of tourists from an idling bus, and so I looked over Paris free of charge. I saw my thief, the yellow dog, full of baguette, slink past the funicular. Then I elevated my gaze to the tapestry of the modern city and reflected on her turbulent history, zealots of various convictions turning blood-mad, sweeping through the avenues without mercy. The revolutionary courts, the guillotine, the SS. And where, I wondered, was Pascal? In the Bastille? Did it still exist? And how could his father turn against him so completely while offering me, in his next breath, meticulous advice on the care of African violets? He had seven such plants potted on his windowsill, four more than he had children.

I left Sacré-Coeur. I backtracked through the ninth and

the second arrondissements. I was lost one moment, found the next. Finally I was back to the lengthening shadows of Notre-Dame, then to Rue Budé. The concierge, upon spying me, scrambled to her feet. Bent over by arthritis, she crab-walked my way and blocked the entrance. Her head came to the level of my chest. "Young sir," she said, "I have opened your apartment to the police. Four of them, with a battering ram. But for me, the door would be in splinters. They left, twenty minutes ago, with parcels."

At the word *police*, my breath was taken from me. "Pascal, it must be about him," I said.

"Pascal? They already have Pascal. They said to me, calling me *old woman*, report any students, radicals, keep a list of visitors."

"Madame," I said, "I know nothing of the politics of France."

"So you say, so you say, dear boy."

I detected a ferocious gleam in her eye. She raised both hands and grasped my shirt. "I am with you, my sympathies are the same as those of my fallen husband. Freedom for Algeria!"

I was in deep water, I could see. I pried myself loose and made for the stairway, forgetting to activate the timer-switch that controlled the lights to the third floor. Darkness therefore followed me step by step as I progressed upwards, as though trouble were tracking me, hard on my heels. The door to our apartment was ajar, but nothing seemed to be disturbed inside. Not in the hallway or the kitchen, the living room, the dining room. But in the bedroom Pascal and I had shared for several nights, there were changes. His books were piled on the dresser, rather than neatly stored on shelves. Several shirts had fallen to the floor of the closet. More germane to me, my passport had moved from the upper drawer of my bedside table to the small desk, pinned under the base of the lamp.

The visitors were telling me something. They knew me, they were watching. And, I thought, I would pay immediate attention. I was the exact opposite of a revolutionary. I would go to the police in the morning and explain myself. Phone home for advice? My parents would laugh, disbelieving, and what could they do. I went out to Rue St. Louis and purchased items at a small grocery, two nectarines, a replacement baguette, slices of ham, a firmer cheese. Then I sat by the Seine in softening light as the tourist boats kicked up small waves against the embankment. Dusk solidified the flying buttresses of the church. My situation was unique, but not precarious. I could reassure the authorities. They would say, "*Canadien errant*, go about your language studies."

Returning to the apartment, by chance I passed a *préfecture de police*, but it was closed at that hour. The next morning, however, I was third in line when the doors opened, and soon I was speaking to a uniformed young man, showing him my passport, explaining as best I could the hornet's nest into which I feared I had fallen. At the word "Algeria," which I could not avoid, his interest perked up. He left and returned in ten minutes. "Be on your way," he said. "There is no record of a police intervention at 8 Rue Budé, nothing. There is nothing to it." He dismissed me and nodded to the next supplicant.

I was not entirely reassured, but a weight lifted from me. I had demonstrated good intentions. The worst was over, I could resume my blameless life. I set out determinedly in the direction of six o'clock, the exact opposite of my previous day's exploration, crossing the river in a southerly direction. On Rue de la Bûcherie, no more than fifty paces from the bridge, I noticed a bookstore with English titles in its window. I was drawn to it, possibly by homesickness. There I browsed for half an hour before purchasing, with two American Express traveller's cheques, Henry Miller's *Tropic of Cancer*. Also *A Spy in the House of Love*, by Anaïs Nin. Labelled as "Erotica," the books were paired in a display, at twenty-five percent off. I took them in an act of courage that I could never have duplicated at home. Then I left the English bookstore and passed through clusters of students rushing hither and yon. Many were not much older than I. They were holding animated discussions, smoking, waving hands in the air. I walked on, feeling a painful social isolation. Then I came to a tall iron fence composed of metal spears, black with gold tips, surrounding an urban park so vast that its far side was invisible, blocked by crowns of trees. Unfolding my map to place myself, I found a thumbprint of green, Le Jardin du Luxembourg. From the nearest gate, one hundred paces down Rue St. Michel, I entered a manicured promenade, tree-lined on both sides. Pascal must have walked here a thousand times and played as a child. His father, if present, would have been aloof, staring at the sky. Mother and the older sisters, hovering.

I walked deeper into the park, separating myself physically and psychologically from the incessant buzz of the city. I repeated to myself, in English, "the Luxembourg Gardens, the Luxembourg Gardens," feeling those two consecutive hard *g*'s on my palate, drumbeating, syncopated. To my right was a château-like building, possibly a manor house for the grounds, but I was not attracted to it. Instead I turned to the left and followed a wide path that curved away to the southwest. Benches had been placed at intervals throughout the gardens, punctuating the greenery of the lawns, the gravelled paths. I came to one that was unoccupied, dappled in half-sunlight. The bench's seat was much longer than those we had at home, longer than the ones by Grenadier Pond, for example. In fact, these were long enough to stretch out upon and still leave room for others. But at that hour the park was sparsely populated. There was no competition for my place. I sat for two hours transfixed by *The Tropic of Cancer*, lost to Miller's confident prose, to a Paris I could only hope to know, sexually transgressive, boisterous.

Past noon, a light rain began to fall. There was a café not far away but deeper into the park, with chalk-boarded prices. Resident pigeons patrolled the ground for crumbs, but as the place was nearly empty, irritation was evident in the way they bobbed their heads. As for the waiters, they were opening table umbrellas, talking among themselves. When they finally noticed me, I ordered and paid far too much for a tiny bottle of Orangina, a buttery croque monsieur. Then the rain accelerated to a downpour, and I half-sprinted from the Luxembourg Gardens, leaving by the same gate I had entered. Protecting my books by stuffing them under my shirt, I lowered my head against gusts of wind and ran back across the bridge.

At Rue Budé, my concierge made a strange gesture to

me from behind her window, pressing two fingers of her right hand in a V against her left breast. Her lips moved too, but silently, incomprehensibly. To please her, I repeated her hand movements as best I could, and then I stooped to ask, "Has Pascal returned?"

"No, he was a dreamer, Pascal, a nice boy."

A ridiculous thought then came to me, that she was an *agent provocateur*, planted by the police to draw me into some quagmire. I headed up the stairs to the drumming of rain in the courtyard. I resolved to become even more visibly apolitical. In the dim light of a brass lamp, I finished the Miller novel. Its profound effect upon me manifested itself later in the night when, awakening from a dream, I realized I was ejaculating into my underpants, my undershirt, into the bedclothes. I blushed from embarrassment even in the darkness of that unfamiliar bedroom, grateful to be unobserved, grateful that the police with their battering ram were not coming through the door. I heard only the low ticking of the clock in the hallway, a shout from the street. I tried to recapture the sexual imagery, whatever it was, but it was unreachable. In the morning, I hand-washed my sullied clothes in the bathroom sink, hanging them just inside the open window to dry. Then I peeled an orange and separated it into segments. Juice spilled onto my fingers.

Enough of Henry Miller, of Anaïs Nin! I resolved to avoid the English bookstore and read instead from Flaubert, Stendhal, Proust, in the original. I would spend as little money as possible on food. I would live on cans of tuna fish, hard-boiled eggs, baguettes, the cheaper cheeses, fruit and vegetables. I would spend the remaining weeks of my exchange entirely in the sanctuary of the Luxembourg Gardens.

Down the stairs I tiptoed, hoping to avoid the concierge. "Young man!" she said, "please, deliver this for me!" She handed me a grenade-sized package heavily wrapped in brown paper. "Just around the corner, to my sister!" I could not refuse, though perhaps she had asked the same of Pascal. Perhaps he was innocent, a hapless fool, and she a master of deceit.

"Certainly, Madame," I said. It was early, the street was empty. No one could possibly be watching. Whatever I was carrying was received matter-of-factly, two minutes later. Shed of that nervous responsibility, I hurried along the Seine until I came to the bookstalls. There I purchased a much-used copy of *Madame Bovary* and, checking over my shoulder first, I picked up a mimeographed pamphlet, *The French in Algeria*. The author's name had been scratched out on the cover with a sharp instrument. On the title page, equally violently, his identity had been excised with a sharp knife or scissors, leaving a linear gap through which the word *vérité* could be seen. The bookseller raised his eyebrows, shrugged, and threw it in for free.

Satisfied, I set out for the Gardens. My bench was still vacant. I took a closer look at it, intending to describe it on a postcard. Of utilitarian design, it was constructed of a single horizontal plank, ten feet long and six inches wide, painted in forest-green. The backrest was even more spartan, a single two-by-four that pressed between the shoulder blades. The bench did not appear to be comfortable, but it was. Through aging, it bent under me slightly, like a hammock. To both sides were chestnut trees providing shade, leaves rustling in the breeze. I could be happy there, I knew, but first I should be practical. I should learn more about the political situation.

I put *Madame Bovary* aside and opened the damaged pamphlet. An hour later, my head spinning from acronyms—OAS, FLN, GPRA—I thought I had a basic grasp of the situation. France had invaded Algeria in the 1830s, had suppressed the Muslim population, had been accused of genocide. Resistance had predictably formed, violence had spread to continental France. French police were now being targeted as individuals, in and around Paris. War, in other words, was coming to the capital.

I realized that I had picked up an incendiary tract, its author an open supporter of the Communist Party. Leaving Flaubert face-down on my bench, I walked a few steps away and dropped the pamphlet into a waste container. Not mine, I would say, not mine. Then I returned to the novel and became absorbed by it, underlining sections in pencil. I was a student and this was my exchange, not with Pascal, not with his family, but with Flaubert.

Each morning after that I set out for the Luxembourg Gardens, waiting for my time in France to end. I settled eventually on the works of Proust, thinking him apolitical. September edged into October. The leaves of the chestnuts yellowed and fell. I carried a sweater with me, pulling it on and off as required. The office girls who came to the Luxembourg Gardens at lunchtime changed from micro-skirts to warmer, body-hugging attire. As usual, they sat on their own benches nearby, chatting, smoking cigarettes, eating sparingly from paper-bag lunches, paying no attention to me. The same could not be said of my concierge, who invariably jumped up from her station when, at the end of my day, I returned to the apartment. I would be lying if I pretended to remember her exact words, but they were always pointed. "Young man, you are a reader, you should know that Albert Camus is a traitor to the cause." "They are killing policemen, and rightly so. Most of them were Nazi collaborators, the police, their sins washed clean by forgetfulness."

I listened with apparent sympathy. I imagined Pascal doing the same, sealing his fate. "Yes," I said, "yes," and then I would mention the number of days I had left in Paris. I resold my Henry Miller to the bookstore but kept Anaïs Nin at my bedside. Mornings, I walked to the Luxembourg Gardens. I annotated Proust. I stretched out on my bench and fell asleep to the cooing of pigeons, the laughter of the girls, the shuffling steps of old men. Cooler weather brought old soldiers out for a last gasp of air. Casualties of the first war, I assumed, amputees with canes, accompanied by nurses dressed in blue. They shuffled along together, eight or ten at once, shoes or slippers scuffing at crushed stone. I could taste the limestone dust on my fingers as I turned the pages. I observed the ancient warriors but I did not honour, in my heart, their sacrifice. I was distancing myself, preparing for home.

In the second week of October, knowing her time with me was limited, my concierge became even more animated in her commentary. "Young man, if you were dark-skinned, you would not be prancing about the city, carefree." And the next evening, "The French National Police, our Gestapo, have imposed a curfew on all Algerian Muslims!" Finally, "There will be a protest march tomorrow, my Canadian friend, and if my husband were alive, he would be at the epicentre, fist raised."

It was more and more clear to me whom the police should have arrested. I readied my suitcase for a quick departure, slipping my passport into my pocket. On the morning of my last full day, rather than head immediately for the Luxembourg Gardens, I decided to bookend my Parisian experience with a repeat trip to Sacré-Coeur. This time, as my pocket money had held out, I would pay for the funicular. I bought a larger sandwich, to share with the dog. I stood for five minutes beneath the gargoyles of Notre-Dame, noticing how eroded some of them were, pockmarked by weather. Then I crossed to the Right Bank but only made it halfway to my goal. A wall of policemen blocked every street. Beyond them I could see the homemade signs of Algerian marchers, slowly advancing. Signs in French against racism, signs in Arabic.

I turned briskly, wanting no part of it. To dislocate me further, all the benches in my favourite area of the Luxembourg Gardens were taken, forcing me closer to the café. There I read throughout the afternoon. For lunch, I ate the dog's portion of the sandwich, for dinner my own.

The sun slipped low enough to cast long shadows, then dusk fell, then the cumulative exhaust of motor vehicles weighed down the air. Three black men ran past me, an unusual sight in the Luxembourg Gardens. They were headed in the direction of the river. I was reluctant to move but would have to follow them before long. I said goodbye to the pigeons not already gone to roost, to the bench that had welcomed me. Goodbye, Luxembourg Gardens. But some sort of melee was spilling back through the streets by the Seine. Sirens and flashing lights forced me away from the Pont St. Michel. Then there were two bodies on the street, smears of blood leading up to them as though they had been dragged there and dropped. Onlookers in clusters, not particularly concerned. They would have said the same of me, for I quickly sidestepped and made for the Petit Pont, one hundred yards to the east. From there I could see bodies being thrown from the Pont St. Michel to the river. I looked the other way. I picked up my pace to the apartment, past the cathedral again, the empty square, empty streets, another bridge, also empty. My concierge was gone too, and she was absent the next morning when I dropped the key on her desk.

In Toronto, my parents were alarmed and disappointed. Paris, the height of civilization! Pascal, not to our surprise, never showed up for his leg of the exchange. A decade later I realized—after the FLQ, after Baader-Meinhof, after Augusto Pinochet—that Pascal had acquitted himself much better than I, in the summer of 1961. He had stood up for, or been victimized by, a principle, while there I was, living in his stead, tending his father's plants, reading Flaubert, reading Proust, marginally improving my French, shrinking into myself in the Luxembourg Gardens.

THE GLASS FLOWERS

HERE, IN THE BOTANICAL Museum, in Cambridge, Massachusetts, in a vast room accompanied by the low hum of humidifiers, are the four thousand glass-and-wire constructs known as the Glass Flowers, each of which is of such delicacy as to seem to breathe from within its cabinet of glass; here, for example, is just a common kind of grass lying on its side as though pulled from the earth, roots tangled and clustered and as wayward as such roots are, twisted and hung with gravity, and the green of the blades is as varied and imperfect as the green of nature; here are scarlet maple leaves, indistinguishable (though these leaves will never change) from those we shuffle through in autumn; here is the elegant pitcher plant from Newfoundland, which drowns insects for its sustenance; here is the saprophytic Indian pipe, dead-white and cold and shrivelling black when it dies; here are the lilies and the orchids, the celebratory laurel, the gentian, the iris and the pomegranate, all of them, one by one, created by Leopold and Rudolf Blaschka between 1887 and 1936 in Dresden, Germany, at that time the most beautiful city in Europe, and so it remained until February 1945, when thousands of tons of incendiary bombs fell from the night sky and the temperature at ground level approached 2,500 degrees Celsius, sucking oxygen from those who tried to breathe in their sheltered rooms and basements and gardens, and the ash of Dresden bone mixed with the sandy loam and blew hot with the blast-furnace heat of revenge and coarse slabs of glass, crude glass as black as obsidian, flowed over flowers.

MARRIAGE STORY

RECENTLY MY WIFE AND I attended a play—*Straight Line Crazy*—at the Bridge Theatre in London, starring the actor Ralph Fiennes, and Ralph Fiennes put on such a dominating performance that we joined in the standing ovation as the curtain fell, although to be accurate there was no curtain, the ending was announced by a brightening of houselights and by simultaneous changes in the postures of the actors, relaxing, holding hands stage-centre, bowing in unison, and afterwards, satisfied but not as transported by the experience as we had hoped, we walked in darkness to the nearest street corner, to a bus stop, and within five minutes, during which no bus appeared, all foot traffic in the area also vanished, leaving us alone, curiously alone in such a populous city usually thronged with crowds past midnight, and the street-lights east and west of us seemed dimmer than those elsewhere, encouraging overlapping pools of darkness to advance upon us as we waited, as we discussed the strengths and weaknesses of the play we had just seen, scanning also, as we did so, the distant, empty one-way street, waiting for the anticipated bus, until lo and behold a solitary figure walked toward us from the direction of the Bridge Theatre, not using the narrow sidewalk, stepping instead down the middle of the street, casually, in no haste, until he was but a few feet away and we saw that it was Ralph Fiennes entirely without the trappings of stage or stardom, without limousine or hangers-on, surprisingly short in stature, wearing common jeans and a leather jacket and a backpack, leaving the environs of the Bridge Theatre as an ordinary citizen for, perhaps, the nearest Tube station, and his pace was such that he did not hurry by, in fact he looked directly at us, intently, slowing down, so that Cheryl and I instantly felt that we were actors ourselves, in a new play without script or audience, and so we felt free in the sudden night to speak up despite our natural shyness, to say hello, to literally thumbs-up Ralph Fiennes' performance, and to our pleasure he stopped and spoke to us as though he were as familiar with us as we were with him, perhaps because, we postulated later, laughing, he must have noticed us in the audience at the Revue Cinema, in Toronto, in 1997, when he loomed high above us on the silver screen for two hours in the Ondaatje-Merchant-Ivory film *The English Patient*, but whatever the reason for his friendliness on that night in London, after exchanging pleasantries he wished us good night, good night, before moving on, becoming smaller, smaller, gone, until we realized that no bus would ever come for us, and so we followed in his footsteps, found the London Bridge Tube station, returned to our hotel in Southwark, stopped in the bar for a drink, and Cheryl turned to me and said that another famous man's gaze had passed over us in a similar fashion, hadn't it, just as we had experienced an hour before with Ralph Fiennes, and I agreed with her yes, yes, remembering the magical time within an even more dramatic setting than the desolate avenue from which we had just departed, so we asked the waiter for a second glass of wine despite the lateness of the hour, despite the staff desultorily shifting chairs and polishing glasses, we delayed paying the modest bill and taking the silent, mirrored elevator to the fifth floor, to the swirl-carpeted hall, the card key, the sensor, the pushing open of the heavy hotel door, we delayed ripping off the duvet and falling upon each other, passion undiminished by familiarity, instead we allowed the small candle floating in water between us to flicker, gutter, sway as we reminisced about our Director from the Space

Institute, a very different man than Ralph Fiennes because the latter was of course a celebrity, a known commodity with whom we had managed to build, however fleeting, the scaffolding of a relationship, whereas neither Cheryl nor I had any knowledge of the Director when first we met, no idea of his international importance when by chance our paths crossed in Italy, and although we were much impressed at the time, in the fire of our youth and self-obsession he became only an interesting anecdote until, from the first row of the auditorium, at the Space Institute in Bern, years later, we realized that we had already met him, physicist exemplar, master of exit velocity and trajectory, charged with planning, if possible, humanity's eventual escape from this bruised and burning planet, and he recognized us too, we saw and felt the millisecond pause as his gaze swept over us, and I even felt a draft, as though a door had opened and closed somewhere on the empty balcony above, thrusting me, thrusting us back to the waterfront at Nice, in France, the day Cheryl and I first met, both of us nineteen, among a ragtag crew hired for the morning to clean up the Promenade des Anglais in front of the Hotel Le Negresco, a celebration of some kind the night before having left tattered remnants of fireworks scattered about, spent rockets, charred and twisted sparklers, torn paper from fist-sized firecrackers, how in the course of our duties we were attracted to each other and stayed together for the long hours of a summer afternoon, rollerblading the waterfront as far as the airport and back, climbing the hill overlooking the Mediterranean, shopping for oranges, riding trolley cars from Place Masséna, and we even made it as far as the Matisse Chapel, high up a grinding bus ride into the flower-bedecked suburb of Venice before sleeping platonically together in a small park, tucked under a hedge in our sleeping bags, and in the morning we set out, hitchhiking, for the youth hostel in Menaggio, north of Milan, to the storied waters of Lake Como where, several days later, in a borrowed punt, rowing side by side, each with an oar, we attempted to re-enact Tennyson's poem, the one that begins "Row us out from Desenzano," but we forgot the words, the lake was dead flat, becalmed, the mountain range to the north etched into the water as perfectly as in a painting by Canaletto, a rare phenomenon, we later learned, but one that explained the lone sailor we spied in mid-distance, marooned, sail collapsed, his rudimentary dinghy stalled, every molecule of surrounding water and air in paralysis, so captivating a diorama that we put aside our budding fascination with each other, our physical attractions, and we worried instead that he might not reach safe harbour before darkness so we altered our course, shifting our weight, rubbing shoulders provocatively as we dipped and pulled in synchrony for five minutes, ten minutes until we reached the vessel, one of simple design, of wood painted white with a single mast, no more than twelve feet in length, with no means of propulsion, and shore was so far away that we offered him a tasselled tow-rope, holding it high, gesturing, suggesting in a mixture of French and English that he affix it to his bow, an offer politely declined by the middle-aged man in shorts and T-shirt who was leaning comfortably, unconcerned, against the port gunwale, tiller unattended, thanking us for our solicitude but declining assistance, saying that he was familiar with the idiosyncrasies of Lake Como, that if we looked closely to the north, where already the sky was turning gold and magenta, we would see plumes of snow lifting from the most distant peak, plumes generated by Alpine winds that would soon fill his sail and carry him safely to Bellano by midnight, therefore he lacked nothing, we could confidently leave him where he was, so we did, we rowed away no longer concerned, content that we had performed a generous act even if rebuffed by that very impressive man, so composed, grave in his demeanour yet accepting of our naïveté, our ignorance of the weather patterns of Lake Como, and indeed soon the predicted winds were ruffling Cheryl's hair and mine, wavelets were beginning to push us eagerly toward shore, we bobbed occasionally in the wake of passing motor vessels but behind us we could see, with gratitude, the independent mariner's sail snap at the sheets, then fill, and his tiny boat began to move at right angles to ours across the darkening waters of the lake, which were no longer touched directly by the sun although the evening sky, high above, remained as rich in colour as any woven tapestry, and that was the memory I knew we were sharing, Cheryl and I, as we recognized our sailor, just as he recognized us among the twelve Candidates at the Institute in Bern, we saw the millisecond pause as he scanned our faces, and it was only human nature for us to wonder, then and later, if our chance meeting on Lake Como might affect our status as Candidates, would it offer us an advantage, a leg up, or would it do the opposite, did we even wish to think in such crass terms, did we want to be chosen after all, these chaotic thoughts tumbling against each other as we listened to the Director describe an autopsy he had performed after an accident on the Autobahn, a lorry from Copenhagen loaded with iron ore sliding sideways on road-slick and driver fatigue into the path of a Toyota Yaris, shunting the tiny car first into the walled median before it became airborne at the same moment that the airbag, powdered for preservation, burst forth from its engineered cell, nitrogen gas exploding volumetrically by a thousand times, cracking ribs, shattering glasses, expelling dentures, compressing the liver to half-size, thunder-slamming against rib cage and spine, a terrible energy release, he said, but nothing compared to what we as Candidates might expect from the G-force necessary to escape this troubled organism, Gaia, Earth, an escape for which we had been prepared by multiple simulations, by physical training and mental hardening before we would be strapped into leather harnesses and cushioned chairs, pinned like butterflies into thrust and momentum beyond imagination, shot from hypermodern cannons, and so on, and so on, he said nothing that was news to us or terrifying, he was speaking over our heads to the international press corps until at last he took a folded piece of paper from his pocket and announced, without further fanfare, without a second glance in our direction, his final decision for the successful Candidates, choosing two others, reasonable choices some might say, passing us over despite our elite accomplishments, as though he were privy to our private thoughts, our mutual hesitation, as though he remembered Lake Como, the tasselled rope, the plumes of snow, the magenta sky, as though he loved us more than he loved his Programme and would keep us forever bound to Earth, as though he could foresee, for us, not the details—Ralph Fiennes, for example, the London street, the swirl-carpeted hall, the card key, the duvet thrown to the floor—but the humdrum essence of the life he wanted us to have, our marriage, our children, the metronomic passage of time, the *tick-tock tick-tock* years consumed by trivialities and small disasters, the gamut of emotions commensurate with family life jigsawed onto the crust of this dying planet from which, he knew, no one, no animal, vegetable, or mineral, ever really wanted to escape.

DUPONT STREET

WE WERE LIVING IN a house on Dupont Street. Bats clustered in the attic, squeaking like door hinges, rustling like crushed cellophane, clambering around, leather wings folded, crawling in tight quarters. They're *crepuscular*—meaning active at dusk and dawn—so we could hear them if there was no wind, we could hear their murmurings, their bat palaver jibbering down through microscopic cracks in the plaster, through the high crown mouldings in Florence's room, over her bed, over her desk, over the 60-watt lamp with the pull-toggle made of brass, her pillows, her pyjamas tossed to the floor, the posters she liked. We coexisted, but it was inevitable, from time to time, that one of those bats would get lost or venture out upon some mission we couldn't understand, and it would drop down from the ceiling, and at times like those we'd be filled with a kind of electricity hard to describe, we'd jump and run and swing ineffective badminton racquets into the swivelled and jacked-up air until it tired from its exertions and fell to the floor. Then we'd throw blankets over it, pin it down, feel it surrender, and we'd call on Florence to wrap it up, carry it outside to the street, shake it out like laundry. Off it would go to some other roofline, eave or soffit, to some pliable entry-point we never could see. Hard to remember, looking back, how many bats we had together as a family on Dupont Street. Then of course Florence left, she finished school, went to Montreal, rented cheaply on Rue Ste. Famille, met certain kinds of friends, worked at a late-night restaurant, called us on Sundays to say hello. And the bats? They were still there under the crown moulding. They could have been dangerous, rabid, but they never touched any of us despite the proximity we shared. We coexisted, as I said before, almost like family on those days and nights—especially the nights—when we could hear them shuffling behind the cracks in the plaster, murmuring over Florence's bed, over her desk, her pillows, her pyjamas thrown to the floor, the lamp with the pull-toggle made of brass, while downstairs there we were, you and I murmuring too, in the kitchen, coffees half-spilled cold into saucers, thinking to ourselves, *what the hell, what the hell? it's past two in the morning … three … four* until the sun came up and there we were, still waiting for a car door, for footsteps, for anything, for her, for Florence, you and I and our bats jammed together on Dupont Street, the bats getting more sleep than we were, all of us, all of us, all of us living in Florence's thrall.

GENETIC MEMORY

WE MET ON DUPONT STREET in a spring blizzard, snow coming down aslant, and after that whatever you had fell apart, you left your husband, we took custody of your three-year-old son and drove north of Superior, camped through the prairies, up the Alaska Highway, getting closer, jammed together in the van twenty-four hours a day, four thousand miles to the Klondike River, islands of tossed gravel, broken trees, destruction wrought upon the riverbed, placer mines named Bonanza, Eldorado, Hunker, Bear, men moiling for gold, diesel, backhoe, pressure-sluicing, veins of quartz and gold escaping in all directions.

In Dawson City we sat on wooden sidewalks by the dance hall and reflected on our relationship to the spinning world, animal, vegetable, mineral, Gaia, David Suzuki, *The Whole Earth Catalogue*, *Harrowsmith*, outdated technologies, the showpiece locomotive, the paddlewheeler, dredges tilted sideways on their own extrusions, the wooden Bank of Commerce, Robert Service, Midnight Dome, hodge-podge of streets, the entire modern town of seven hundred, around the bend, Moosehide, Tr'ondëk Hwëch'in, salmon prized over gold.

Deceptively smooth the Yukon River, wrinkled with eddies, glacial-cold, scouring down from the St. Elias Range of mountains through broad-shouldered valleys to the Bering Sea, flow rate 227,000 cubic feet per second, twice that of the Mississippi, the ferry crossing twenty-four hours a day, flat-bottomed, rusted steel, capacity six cars, engine churning, grinding, spinning three-quarters of a circle downstream before pushing to the far side, prow slamming down on mud and grass and there we were, our van, our few contained possessions, to the east the Ogilvie Range, to the west, Alaska.

Alpine barrens, home of the marmot and the grizzly bear, gentian, bog-laurel, rose and poppy, yellow petals pressed between pages of your notebooks, fingerprints of pollen and road-dust, DNAs intertwining, two hours to the low bridge over the Fortymile River, girders there painted as blue-green as the midnight sky, never fully darkening in those high summer days.

Clinton Creek, company town, chrysotile asbestos, pale-white feathers dipping and rising like moths in currents of air, our aluminum half-trailer cinder-blocked for uncertainty high on a wildflower ridge, crocus, lupin, spruce forest falling away to a glint of river, grayling, bears in the back-country, bears in the yard, naïveté on our part as we placed decorative rocks of dishevelled asbestos on our bedside tables, vacuuming snowflakes of chrysotile as they drifted to the floor, seven miles away tailings from the open-pit mine crushed into the boreal forest, a grey-white avalanche of pseudo-snow hardening to the consistency of plaster, never melting, implacable, snapping trees in half, rerouting brooks and creeks and rivulets, smothering underbrush, the refined asbestos carelessly poured into bags, placed on pallets, trucked out of Clinton, broken out at construction sites in Tacoma, Tokyo, Taiwan.

Rogue fibres hitched rides on inspired air, tricking the genome, slivering into cells of lungs, throats, ovaries, twisting the helix, mitosis, cancer, mesothelioma, asbestosis, scientists, politicians, businessmen, accountants, too much evidence to ignore, after two years the mine was closed, our one-purpose extractive town depopulated to zero.

Whitehorse, White Pass, Skagway, BC Ferries, Prince Rupert, 'Ksan, Prince George, Medicine Hat, Sleeping

Buffalo, Bismarck, Fargo, Detroit, Montreal, an upstairs two-bedroom apartment, marriage, Schwartz's, St. Viateur, St. Laurent, Ste. Catherine, Lewis Furey, Carole Laure, *Fantastica*, transit strikes, pregnancy, we were fully re-urbanized until one morning over breakfast we opened the *Montreal Gazette* and read that the Porcupine herd of caribou had migrated across the Yukon River for the first time in seventy-five years, propelled—so a naturalist said—by genetic memory, a survival mechanism implanted in DNA, dormant for five caribou generations, and although many had drowned, hundreds of bloated bodies bumping up against sandbars as far downstream as Eagle, Alaska, fifty thousand of the herd survived to clamber ashore at the abandoned first settlement of the gold rush, Fortymile.

Stressors north of 60 for caribou: tapeworm, lungworm, brucellosis, warble fly, slow exsanguination from the bites of a hundred million black flies and mosquitoes, wolves in packs, grizzly bears, frostbite, spring avalanche, golden eagles, pipelines, hunters on ATVs and snowmobiles, chemicals dribbled on highways, methane vaporizing from taiga, wildfire, deforestation, insecticides tasting like burnt rubber when fogged like mustard gas through the seven streets of Clinton Creek.

Phenomena inserted into the human genome by the

experience of our ancestors: the collision of neutron stars, a billion years of buckling of the earth's crust, asteroid hits, the sound of calving icebergs, déjà vu, nostalgia, migrainous auras, epilepsy, foreboding, firepits, arrowheads, Darwinian adjustments, behaviours otherwise inexplicable including self-destructive practices, acts, delusions.

Fortymile, it was our habit when skiing there from Clinton Creek to separate in the twilight darkness of midafternoon, encircle the mostly intact cabins, approach each other and interlock skis, touch foreheads at thirty-five below, ice-encrusted our balaclavas, silent the stars, a thousand miles of snow on every side, *arpents de neige*, aurora borealis snapping audibly against the northern sky, ice cracking, willow branches cracking, thermos of tea frozen.

In Montreal, reading the news, we felt at one with the Porcupine herd of caribou, acknowledging wryly that our genetic memory seemed to be next to zero but theirs was locked in, forged by a thousand years of scraping at permafrost, bog, barren, lichen, moss, lingonberry, one four-legged shaman or wizard lifting her head and, shivering brain-afire, stepping into the mica-filled current, the whisper-whispering of it, fifty thousand following her, and how surprised they must have been to see the changes wrought at Fortymile since last they visited, log cabins desiccated by the desert heat of Yukon summer, charred by lightning-strike, by human carelessness, sod roofs collapsed, doorways bent and cracked, how high the grass and thistle had grown, slow the bees in goldenrod and saxifrage, tangled the rose, unchanged the whiskeyjack, the raven, the cicada, the line of shoreline alders as they stepped fastidiously upstream through shallow rapids to Clinton Creek, to the soccer pitch we left behind, the baseball field, the arena scraped to permafrost, school dismantled, houses hauled away, browsing for days puzzled but unconcerned, passing our trailer site where the crocus and lupin flower had been, for us, spring-loaded, high above that river of gold.

Our baby had colic. We took turns walking the floor, holding him as he cried past midnight, slow-dancing, his unhappy chest on yours or mine, neighbours unable to sleep, banging fists against the adjoining wall. Sorry, sorry, we said inaudibly as outside muffled plows moved through drifts, through otherwise-impassable streets, snow falling on the mediaeval turrets of the hospital where you gave birth, on the English poets of Crescent Street, on Joyce's living and the dead, snow falling even deeper east of St. Laurent where French was spoken so rapidly we could not understand, snow on troubadours singing in praise of winter, on the election of the Parti Québècois, Côtes des Neige a blur of white horizontal, and in the vestibule of our apartment we brushed snow from our clothes as once we brushed asbestos. We walked upstairs, cooked dinner, read books to the children, put them to bed, turned off the lights as snowsqualls, flurries, blizzards laced the windows, 2426 Park Row West, sirens from Sherbrooke Street reverberating to some local, personal vulnerability.

Floorboards creaking, slow-dancing, sorry, sorry, our species' dire concerns, the moratorium on cod, draggers, clear-cuts, sewage, whatever else we have done to North America since 1492, the Porcupine herd a signifier, Rachel Carson, silent spring, our children's children herded together forty years from now, standing by some turgid, stinking river green with algae, mist on the lowlands, waiting dumbfounded for a signal to cross.

GRATING

I CAN SEE WHY someone might like it here, comparatively it's warm, and there's a hum, a vibration, a rush from below that has real force behind it, you can feel it on your socks, your pant legs, banks of industrial fans going twenty-four hours a day, trains in tight tunnels fifty-five feet below sucking commuter sweat and urban body-ooze from wool, rubber, polyester—mind the gap—much like syringes draw blood, vacuum-drawn samples of regret, exhaustion, anticipation, foreboding, nostalgia, déjà vu, misused pharmaceuticals, unidentifiable vapours and aerosols escaping through engineered slits in tiled walls and ceilings, through plastic and aluminum hosing, baffles, vents, angulated shafts welded into infrastructure until this one forced exit, these thin metallic bars, this grating recessed one-quarter inch into the sidewalk outside Dundas Station, flurries of snow soaking flats of cardboard, rough accommodation, no door, no threshold, no walls, but I wonder, tasting it on my tongue, this effluent, how long can anyone breathe it in, it's metallic, it's ionized, it's third-rail electricity smashing molecules of steel, axle grease, lottery tickets, N95s, damp newspapers, sputum, urine, spinning off wheel trolleys past advertising panels for lipstick, musicals, dog food, past digital clocks, up-down escalators, late-night stragglers until at last those two spinning vortices, those giant fans, Scylla and Charybdis working non-stop, eating at hoarfrost on winter nights like this but it's toxic, it has to be, look at the people about to lie down in this neon cul-de-sac, look at their eyes, their nostrils, their hair.

KNIGHT ERRANT

MY SISTER HAS KEPT my talisman, a ribboned medal won at darts in Liverpool, 1978.

I am an ungainly figure, clad in mail. A stirruped foot, a machine for the saddling. Ropes, pulleys, some laughter, but it was done like this long before electricity.

Each tiny circle of mail is coupled to four others. It enslaves me to my lance. Sun shimmers, Roanoke groans and turns. His unusual musculature. His fetlocks, hocks, and shanks once flawless, now edematous.

The director, whose father came from Turkistan, values "fluid grace." His assistant carries a clipboard, her sweater wired for sound.

I have taken Roanoke from his field, the sea at his feet. His hooves are as heavy as waffle irons, turning furrows in the sand.

Razor wire, bales of straw, longbows, the catapult. Halberds. My visor is built for deflecting blows. Our targets were straw in burlap, grain burst to the ground.

Drones overhead from the White House, their last-minute buzzings.

Camel, horse, pony, cart, caravan: all are sought out by the eye adamant.

Once upon a time they wore the moon half-crescent and were called Saracen.

Shell Oil has placed one of its signs on the horizon. A yellow half-bivalve. Venus de Milo. Oil sponges from under our feet, like warm marzipan.

Water, figs, grapes, an oasis. They sell postcards showing it thus.

Roanoke twitches his ears. A battlefield, so flies are at home, bluebottle, iridescent aerated through gauze, labels saying Hanoi, Nevada, Guadalcanal.

Moths as white as lilies beat against screens. Powdered, their wings arsenic. Mosquitoes home in on contrails of carbon dioxide, malarial.

Google: Hugh Thompson, the Viet Cong, the fusillade. Icarus. The Brownian movement of dust.

We are to be mortal enemies, yet during the breaks we share a Fresca.

The hotel in Dubai. We can afford it with our danger pay. The shade of underground garages, the cool, the damp. Roanoke and a Ferrari, side by side.

Some of the German officers wear lightning flashes. Their walkie-talkies bristle with command.

The key grip, the gaffer, the mixer, unshod Arabians. Dispatch boxes, carrier pigeons, Navajo interpreters.

Beech trees flown in from Byelorussia, half-grown from flesh. Swarthy the faces of extras, ultrafine the shifting grains of sand.

Wind scrapes the surface like shedding snakeskin, a crickling like spent electricity. Camels, their teeth as large as piano keys, rip at baled eucalyptus.

Bodies of legionnaires have been propped in the parapets, a shimmering, a mirage for those without technology.

Hot the asphalt, parking stripes smeared like the yolk of eggs, griddled.

In My Lai they lost their minds.

Arabs came to his parents' shop in LA, where they bought figs. He went to film school in Santa Barbara. He owned a Nikon, a Super 8, his project a wall, whitewashed, pocked with ricochet.

Her nails are split from the heat, the aridity. They catch in the nap of her sweater. She wears her iPhone in what she mistakenly calls a "*sac-à-main*," on a cord around her neck.

Pomp and circumstance, something we understand. The Queen, Prince Philip, the slow march. Laredo, the Ghost Dance. Our weapons too are anachronistic, on loan from the museum.

Twice daily he Skypes to faces reflected in mahogany.

Poppies blow. Listening devices, the Ottoman Empire built on spice and glass.

Haystacks of dollars, euros, Swiss francs bulldozed onto trains bound for Marseille, Málaga, Gibraltar, Torremolinos.

Celluloid combusts in sunshine. The open well sucks dry. Contractors from Córdoba drive it down another three hundred metres, dropping pennies to a copper dissonance.

No one thought of the Coen brothers. Someone visually like Philip Glass, they said.

Glenn Gould insomniac, his breathing audible at 2:53, 3:11, etc., etc. Night vision, Antietam, Vietnam, *A Midsummer Night's Dream*.

Three Jeeps burn on the outskirts of Tripoli. Black smoke smudges the sky to Sicily, to Monte Cassino, to a lamppost in Milan. Mussolini and Claretta Petacci, her skirt awry. Bloodthirsty the leering multitude, in black and white.

Announcement: German women will take care of the cast children tonight, in the compound provided.

The English have seconded Roanoke. I run through the underground garage.

The director burns his hands. The Coleman stove, a micro-crack in the pressure valve, a spray of fuel. Second-degree, she says. He coats each finger with Vaseline, then wraps them in strips of muslin. Edward Scissorhands, he says, holding them up. No, Ozymandias, King of Kings.

Dry as papyrus, the air inside. Static crackles from her sweater, tiny sparks, her hands and elbows moving overhead.

Typhoid rampant in the barracks. Turnips flown in from Poland barely cooked. Behind triple fencing: kapos, dirt, weeds, a roll call with absentees. Sirens from Santiago, Chile.

Rwandans. They huddle by the coffee truck. Beans there are ground as fine as dust. Water simmers in a pan aluminum.

Phosphorus. Mustard gas. Uranium-235.

By the slaughterhouse, cattle are lowing.

I find Roanoke, his nostrils flaring. He has refused to ride into the Valley of Death. Pillboxes, Russian shooters picking their teeth, waiting. Bren guns swivel, an explosion of blackbirds.

The sun is at its zenith and I am soakèd through. Glistening too are the hides of animals. The water trough is cracked, empty, sandpapered by the tongues of reptiles, excoriated.

Cellphones smashed with hammers. The crew's disconsolate, dehydrated, spouting nonsense.

He's lost his Seroquel, tumbled it to the floor. All she has for him is aspirin, quinine, the last ice cube. He sees ayatollahs in black, canteens hoarded, their index fingers in the air.

Prophets. The Annunciation. The Vatican. William T. Vollmann, the Jesuits in Quebec.

Khartoum, Cameroon, dementia, desert fever. Scorpions under petrol cans quicker than lizards. Days of waterboarding, nights of Metallica. A minaret at sunrise, faux plywood shredded by jihad. The muezzin call. Three speedboats just in case, on speed-dial, sequestered, tarpaulined in Cairo, under the bridge Qasr al-Nil.

We are bivouacked in a white tent scalloped corner to corner, cornice to cornice. A pinnace up high, a fluttered bird. At the far end, Roanoke and three goats, the latter now hobbled, stepping in circles.

We make passes before a "festive audience." Men indentured from the Philippines push against barricades. With high-tech mirrors, CGI, food colouring rubbed on by grooms, Roanoke and I become six.

My lance has been openly sabotaged. Micro-cuts in

bamboo. An expert with an adze, hired for the weakening.

Beyond the circled trucks, Apache teach the Saracen invisibility. Part peyote, part skill. Their faces are painted in chalk, in ochre, gouache, bunker crude, anything to diminish the effects of light.

The Germans and the Japanese play at beach volleyball. R and R. Joyous are their voices, each anticipating victory.

Her hand is on Roanoke's shoulder. SPF-60, Chanel, slightly freckled, sunglasses mirrored to blue. There's a rent in the fabric of your mail, she says, curiously, fingering it.

She riffles through pages of the script, as it was before changes. I hear the wings of dead insects, rustling. Take me with you when you go, she says.

Garlands in your hair. Lovely. My voice is muffled, my masque of iron.

The desert has taken his intelligence. Squinting, he sees a jouster on a horse, monstrous. He fumbles for the field telephone, bends to it, the wooden box. Cranks the handle. Houston, Houston, he says. A toy helicopter, flying it by hand. Saigon, blades like cleavers, like bumblebees, a klaxon saying diplomats, next of kin, spies, wholesalers, concubines, in that order. Pandemonium on the rooftops.

Storyboards! Montage! Film every sector at once, find me my chair. His voice interpreted in seven languages.

Robots on GPS. Cameras scan, rolling through grit, sand, grind, WD-40, a certain amount of fingertip-skilled cajolement.

Sector One: Amsterdam 1943, the canal. Steps on the stairs, a knocking. Soundtrack: a girl's heartbeat: 60, 70, 80, 110, 140, 150. Pogrom, the marking of doors.

Sector Two: A dark-haired man from Belfast miscast as Suleiman. He proposes to divide the child. Courtiers, *aides-de-camp*, ladies-in-waiting, a fine spray from shower heads, perfume crushed from seeds of pomegranate.

Sector Three: Letters home full of bravado. The Japanese are many islands away, retreating. Comfort women, ankles tied to cots, linen strips recycled from bandages. Shadows succumb, hurricane lamps sputter low on kerosene. Samurai, their swords going *lop* through cantaloupe.

Sector Four: Politicians pushed to the front line, armed with daggers. Rancid their sweat, their non-physicality. Escape hatches open and close to the garden at Versailles. Emissaries from Halliburton, suits, computers, bodies BMI>30 pour from the hotel like predatory ants.

Sector Five: Tumbrels, cobbles, the knitting of names. Cars in Omagh blown by rosaries, by the colour Orange. Genghis Khan, early-morning Mongolian chill. French army in retreat, their bayonets discarded for weight. The well at Cawnpore. Highland clearings, bagpipes shredded like sheep. IEDS. Blankets with smallpox, accepted.

Sector Six: Partisans fire guns in the air. Counter-partisans pour from caves. Olive trees, branches pollarded against the snow. Greece or Macedonia, a Brueghel from afar.

Sector Seven: Stukas and F-16s strafe the dunes. Dozens of Apaches caught dead to rights, arrows useless, fletched with the feathers of raven and hawk, ponies half the size of Roanoke. Saracen scattered, "cut to shreds," the Bible, the Koran. Kernels of corn. Buzzards too sated to move.

Sector Eight: German officers smiling, teeth bathed in cyanide, off-green as algae. Shostakovich, whatever he learned in Stalingrad.

Sector Nine: Conning tower, a rolling sea, Fire One, Fire Two, horizon crumples, gel ignited. Oil slick. Sonar, *ping … ping*.

Sector Ten: MASH unit #3, operating room, wounded soldier, bamboo spike in chest, frothing, ticket home.

Sector Eleven: Our first pass. Lances shatter. Lustre on Roanoke's mane a web of roses. His forefeet prance the air. We turn to trumpet, to pipes, a snare, a falcon on a wrist. We charge again and blows are multiplied. Music crescendo, decrescendo, clavichords and krummhorns and the trumpet voluntary. A tremor between my knees.

Smashed kaleidoscope, its circumference pierced. Shards of yellow, green, blue, wrenched into the opposite of clarity.

I offer my glove, she pulls herself up behind. Movie as fucked up as any war, she says. Dervishes, sepoys, machetes, swords, anything that pierces skin.

We slip through the lines. I am Falstaff, Roanoke is Rocinante. The moon on their flag, a fingernail. Orion, the wind sirocco. Hands feather my waist.

In the dunes, we're swaying like a prairie schooner. Sun twisting metal. Bridle made of rope now, strange cries in what might be Japanese or Tagalog, at any rate a foreign tongue, unintelligible.

Roanoke aghast on his side.

The shock of our unseating, this pantomime.

MELTDOWN

DISREGARDING EVERY PRINCIPLE of common sense, we spin through space within our deteriorating biosphere as though we had forever and forever, witnessing the retreat of glaciers from Siberia, Alaska, Antarctica, Greenland, fifty thousand years of history reduced to trickles of silt and water coursing down from ridges, screes, and precipices, from previously protected pockets of sun-shadowed rock and microvegetation, a hundred million tons of snow falling over centuries and by its own weight being crushed to solidity, swallowing history without fanfare, rancor, or prejudice, in remote silence, of duration unimaginable, recording in its pearled density everything that fell from the sky or brushed upon its surface, including evidence of planetary fluxes in orbit and rotation, solar flares, the wax and wane of atmospheric carbon dioxide, nitrogen, oxygen, the accumulation of pollen falling like ochre-yellow smoke, chromosomes settling from pine and oak and cedar, spores from fern and bracken in distinctive layers, season after season plumed into ice, lucky or unlucky insects posing as once they did in amber, layers of ash as ribboned as black letters of death, evidence of cataclysm, subequatorial volcanoes, viral life-forms flash-frozen, plagues patiently waiting for release, ice calving in ominous chunks near Yakutat, bodies of "prehistoric" creatures uncovered, predatory cats with curved incisors, neolithic hunters asleep in crevices with pomaded hair, perfect fingernails, supple skin, clothed in artifacts of leather and wool, ivory tusks of mastodon or mammoth poking from adjacent permafrost recently cleansed by diesel generators, high-pressure hosing, carved by artists into amulets, rings, bracelets, also this bone-white necklace we bought in Dawson City before forever was in doubt, before clear-cuts, methane, reckless winds, floods, tornados, rising sea, starvation, COVID, migration, meltdown.

ACKNOWLEDGEMENTS

THANKS TO EVERYONE AT the House of Anansi for welcoming this book, to Shivaun Hearne, Jenny McWha, and Allegra Robinson for their thoughtful editing, and to Martha Webb at Cooke McDermid Literary Management. Short stories have few outlets in traditional publishing, so I am grateful to the following magazines for creating awards, for reading thousands of entries, for creating deadlines, for celebrating new writing. "Wolverine" (then titled "Mario Vargas Llosa") and "Sweet Boy" both won first prize in the *Exile Quarterly* (Canada) annual competition. "Polio" and "Esther" won first prize in the Bridport International Writing Competition (UK); "George Mallory" won second place in the Flash Fiction category. "The Phosphorescence" was shortlisted for the *Sunday Times* EFG Short Story Award (UK) and appeared in *Brick* literary journal. "Ventimiglia" was shortlisted for the Berlin Prize and published in Germany by Klak Verlag. "Genetic Memory," though written in prose, was shortlisted for *Moth Magazine*'s annual poetry award (Ireland). "Marriage Story" was shortlisted for the CBC Short Story Award. "The Oxford Book of Modern Verse," "Transformation," and "Glass Flowers" were published in *The Irish Pages Press*. "The Luxembourg Gardens" appeared online in TSS Publishing (UK). "Knight Errant" appeared in *Brick* literary journal. The other stories are new to this collection. Thanks to my children too—James, Will, Nora, Jesse—for sharing an enduring love for the written word, the sentence, the paragraph, the story.

© Nathan Saliwonchyk

NICHOLAS RUDDOCK is a physician and writer. Internationally, he has twice won the Bridport International Writing Competition (UK) and has been shortlisted for the *Sunday Times* EFG Short Story Award (UK), the *Moth Magazine* Poetry Award (Ireland), the Manchester Fiction Prize (UK), and the Berlin Prize. In Canada, he has won the *Antigonish Review*'s Sheldon Currie Short Fiction Contest and *Exile* magazine's Carter V. Cooper Award and Nona Heaslip Award. He has also been shortlisted for the Toronto Book Award and the CBC Short Story Award. His latest novel, *Last Hummingbird West of Chile*, was a finalist for the Next Generation Indie Book Awards in 2021. He is married to the artist Cheryl Ruddock and lives in Guelph, Ontario.